The Bells of Freedom

By the author of

HEARTBREAK STREET

WITCH'S SILVER

MASQUERADE

TEN LEAGUES TO BOSTON TOWN

THE
BELLS
OF
FREEDOM

Dorothy Gilman Butters

Illustrations by Carol Wilde

Macrae Smith Company : Philadelphia

To Jonathan

The Bells of Freedom

1

❧ The loft was in deep shadow. Jed lay sprawled in a corner of it, bruised and aching from Silas Clark's whip, and listened to his master complaining of him.

"The boy's ungrateful, lazy, clumsy, muddle-headed and ignorant. I've rued the day I ever hired him out."

The words did not surprise Jed. He had heard them every day for two years and he guessed that he would hear them every day for the next five years, but it no longer mattered. In his twelve years of living Jed had learned to take each day as it came. The important thing was never to think ahead more than a day or two, because another few years of service to Silas Clark was more than anyone could bear.

From the smithy below a man answered. "Where
did you buy him?" The voice was a strange one to
Jed. Men came and went at the smithy and all of
them loved to talk—about horses and politics, the
King, or Silas Clark's ungrateful bound boy.

Silas Clark spat into the dying fire. "Down at
the Long Wharf two years ago. 'E was brought in by
ship from England, and it's my opinion he should ha'
been left there."

"Perhaps the boy would agree with you on
that," said the strange voice dryly.

Jed lifted his head to listen better. Nobody had
ever said that before.

"Proper guttersnipe," sniffed Clark. "Won't
learn. Can't learn. Stubborn."

"How old?"

"Twelve."

"Ah."

"And what's 'ah' mean?" demanded Silas Clark
suspiciously.

"Since he's no good to you it means let's have a
look at him. I could use a boy. If I like the looks of
him I might buy him from you."

Silas Clark said quickly, "I didn't say he was no
use to me."

"No? I thought you did."

Jed chuckled. It didn't matter to him yet that
they were talking about him. It mattered only that
this man—whoever he was—was quick enough and
clever enough to talk back to Silas Clark. Not meanly
—oh no, his voice was smooth and gentle—but none

of Silas Clark's customers had ever cared enough to show their dislike of the man. They talked, they laughed, they paid their money and left. This man was different.

Then it occurred to Jed that the man was talking about him—Jed—and the chuckle died on his lips. He felt oddly frightened.

There was silence in the room below and then Silas Clark suddenly bellowed, "Jed? Jed Crane, come down from the loft and be quick about it."

Jed wiped his eyes with the sleeve of his shirt, sat up, dusted the hay from his breeches and swung his legs over the ladder. He climbed down swiftly, knowing Silas Clark would cuff him if he took too long. At the bottom he turned to look at the man who might need a boy.

The stranger was a short man, comfortably broad in the middle. The first thing Jed noticed about him was the twinkle in his eye, as if he found life amusing. He was also a gentleman, or seemed so beside Silas Clark with his smithy apron and dirty hands. His clothes were of well-cut homespun and his linen was clean. He might be a man who whipped his servants, but there was a brightness and a cheerfulness about him that made Jed feel less frightened.

The stranger, studying Jed in turn, said, "He doesn't look as if he's fed well, Clark, and from the bruise on his cheek you beat him frequently. What's his term of service?"

"Seven years—two of 'em spent," growled Clark.

"Hmm." The bright eyes rested upon Jed's face. "Can you read or write, my boy?"

Jed nervously cleared his throat. "No, sir. But I can print my own name."

"And how did you come to be on a ship docking at the Long Wharf?"

Jed glanced fearfully at Silas Clark but the man only shrugged. "I was stolen, sir," said Jed. "When my mother died I was to go to live with my aunt in Liverpool, but I never reached her house, sir. Three men jumped me in the street and when I came to my senses I was aboard ship for the colonies."

"Kidnapped, eh?" said the stranger thoughtfully. "And how old were you when that happened?"

"Nine, sir—making me twelve this year."

He nodded. "Well, Silas Clark, what price do you put on his services?"

Clark shook his head. "A contract's a contract, Mr. Box. I'd want a fair price."

Mr. Box lifted his eyebrows. "Oh?" he said gently. "But I thought you called him muddleheaded, ignorant and lazy."

Clark flushed. "That I did but I paid twenty pounds for him and he's not given me service worth one pound."

"Ah—then you're well rid of him, are you not?" said this Mr. Box smoothly. "I'll give you ten pounds for him."

"Ten!" bellowed Clark. "That's insulting, sir—insulting, that's what."

"Twelve then."

"Eighteen," said Silas Clark.

Mr. Box's lip curled as if someone had tossed a speck of mud at his white ruffle. "Don't be ridiculous," he said scornfully. "Thirteen, and that's my last offer." To prove it he walked to the door.

Jed watched with a sinking heart. He knew nothing of the stranger except that he was called Mr. Box. But anyone would be better than Silas Clark with his hands like swollen sausages and his temper as hot as his smithy fire. He had scarcely dared hope for a change, but now he realized that he was trembling all over with suspense.

At the door Mr. Box wheeled and said, "Well, Clark?"

Silas tugged at his ear while Jed held his breath. At last he shrugged. "Very well." Having gotten a better price than expected he added spitefully, "He's not worth even that."

Mr. Box's eyes came to rest on Jed. "We'll see about it. Have you paper and pen?"

Silas Clark fetched writing tools and told Jed to get his belongings from the loft. While the two men wrote out the agreement Jed climbed the ladder, feeling more dazed than excited. He was relieved at the thought of going, and yet at the same time uneasy at exchanging what was familiar for something new and strange. Most of all he was surprised that a man like Mr. Box should want a boy who was lazy, ungrateful and clumsy.

Surely there was something strange in that?

Yet he wasn't really clumsy; he knew that. Smithy work demanded strength and muscle, and quick legs and hands, and these he did not have. He was thin and tall for his age, and always hungry. He spent more energy every day than Silas Clark's food gave him back. Being weak made him slow, which brought Silas' fist down upon him and nearly every day the whip. He had learned to be afraid of Silas Clark, and it seemed that fear made a boy even clumsier. He wondered what muscles this new master would demand of him.

Quietly he put together the few possessions he owned: a clean shirt, a rusty jackknife, and the Bible that had been his mother's. He tied these into the spare shirt and descended the ladder.

"Ready, Jed?" His new master was standing by the door.

"Yes, sir." Jed stole a look at Silas Clark and then at the room in which he had been so miserable for two years. He said timidly, "Goodbye, sir."

For answer Silas Clark reached out and took his bundle from him and opened it. He said in a mean voice, "That's to be sure you're not taking what doesn't belong to you. Get along now—and good riddance."

Jed picked up his bundle and walked through the door that Mr. Box held open for him. On the whole, Silas Clark's last words cheered him. His surliness made Jed realize that nothing in his new life could possibly be quite so horrid as what lay behind him.

2

It was a long time since Jed had seen the world outside the smithy, for Silas Clark's son Amos had run the errands. Now he was so eager to look around that he tripped over his new master's heels. "Oh, I beg your pardon!" he gasped.

"Box is the name," said the man. "Titherming Box. Now try to walk with your head to the front, m'boy—it's where God put it."

"Yes, sir," said Jed, falling in behind him.

With huge eyes he gobbled up the sights. It was barely evening in Boston town—six o'clock or so, he guessed by the deepening sky—and there were excit-

ing things to see. The narrow, cobbled street was full
of people: lads like himself scurrying about on errands; plump men in wigs and satin waistcoats stopping to talk to other men in wigs and bright waistcoats; horses clip-clopping over the stones; and
British soldiers in beautiful uniforms, their coats as
red as torches in the twilight. The November sky
was salted with faint stars—the tower of the North
church looked high enough to touch them. As they
crossed State Street Jed looked to the left and caught
a glimpse of the harbor shining like pewter in the
distance. There were shops of every kind to look
into: a wig-maker's, an apothecary's, a hatter's, a
leather-dresser's, a chandler's. Strong in his nostrils
were the smells of a seaside town, of drying fish and
woodsmoke and salt water. Jed sighed with content-
ment.

"This way," said Titherming Box, and Jed fol-
lowed him down a street of tall and narrow buildings.
As these grew closer together Mr. Box's pace slowed.
"Here we are, my boy," he said, drawing out a key.

They had stopped in front of a small shop. A
sign hung over the door, but if Jed could not read
the words on it he could understand the picture—of
an opened book—painted on its boards. He guessed
that Mr. Box was a bookseller or printer. As Mr. Box
unlocked and opened the door a jingle of bells rang
out. Inside there was a pleasing smell that was new to
Jed—of paper and ink, he learned later. A lantern

was lit, and by its light Mr. Box looked at Jed and Jed looked at Mr. Box.

"So," said Mr. Box. "And do you think I've made a mistake in taking you, my boy?" He was regarding Jed with a strange expression. It was as if he asked himself the question instead of Jed.

"Oh no, sir," Jed said eagerly.

"I hope not; I hope not," said Mr. Box. "You've eaten? No, of course you haven't. Supper first and then I'll show you around. . . . You find yourself bound out to a printer and engraver now, my boy."

"Yes, sir," said Jed, his heart lifting at the thought of food. He followed Mr. Box into a long, narrow kitchen at the back. Its hearth-fire had burned out, but by the light of the lantern Mr. Box fetched cheese, bread, a mug of cider and some cold ham. "Eat," he said, pointing to the long trestle table and bench. "From the looks of you, Silas Clark never overloaded your platter."

Jed ate like one who had been starved, his eyes watching Mr. Box closely, for surely there was a flaw to so much kindness. But Mr. Box only sat and looked around the room, drumming his fingers on the rough plank table and frowning.

He said abruptly, "There's nobody to cook for me—I don't like strangers about the house. Your first job will be to cook for me."

"Yes, sir," gasped Jed, his mouth full of bread.

"And don't stuff," said Mr. Box. "Never, *never*

put so much in your mouth you can't speak around
or through it when spoken to."

"Yes, sir—no, sir," said Jed, and swallowed so
much bread at once that his throat hurt.

"You'll go to market every morning and buy the
day's food. You'll run errands for me, delivering
what's printed, and fetching me new ink and paper
when needed. You'll cook and make sure no strangers
hang about. You understand?"

"Is that—all I'm to do?" asked Jed in astonishment.

Mr. Box smiled faintly. "Not quite, but it's
enough for now. Master that and there'll be more."

"Yes, sir."

"Now, if you've finished stuffing yourself I'll
show you the house. Come, come, you can finish the
crumbs later."

Jed leaped to his feet. First, Mr. Box unbarred
the heavy back door and showed him the hogshead
in the garden from which Jed would draw water.
Then the door was barred again and Jed followed his
new master to the front of the building. He had eaten
in the kitchen, which took up the rear of the house.
The shop lay in front of this, with a window opening
on the street. There were two long tables in the
room, one holding what Mr. Box called a rolling
press, the other table piled high with rolls of paper,
pieces of type and a stack of freshly printed handbills.
Jed was to sleep on the long bench under the win-

dow. "So no one can come upon me suddenly in the night," said Mr. Box.

He opened a door in the wall and shone his lantern on narrow, winding stairs. Together they climbed until the stairs divided, one step ending at a door to the right, the other at a door straight ahead. "This," said Mr. Box, opening the door to the right, "is where I sleep. Into this other room," he added, "you're never to go." He held up the lantern and stared at Jed. "Never," he said fiercely. "You understand?"

Jed was startled. "Yes, sir, I understand. But it's got a padlock, hasn't it? Nobody could go in if they wanted to."

"Quite true—unless they stole the key to the padlock. It's on the table beside my bed." Mr. Box led him into the bedroom. "You see?" he said, pointing. "This is the key that unlocks the other room." After they had both stared at it for a few minutes Mr. Box appeared to rouse himself. He fetched a blanket from the cupboard and handed it to Jed.

"There you are. Now go down and fix yourself a bed. You can finish your cheese and ham, too, but mind you clear up afterward."

Jed nodded and said good night. As he descended the stairs alone he heard the bells striking the hour of eight. All over Boston the bells were ringing, some of them loud, some of them soft, but all of them sweet. Jed made short work of tidying up the kitchen. When he lay down on his bench with a hunk of cheese to nibble he could see the stars through the window beside him. He liked that. From somewhere far away he heard the sound of horses' hoofs clattering across cobblestones. In a few hours the Town Watch would begin their rounds for the night, calling out the hour and lighting up the dark streets with their lanterns. A person never felt alone in Boston town.

Jed drew up his blanket. He thought of Mr. Box, and when he remembered the locked room upstairs he could not keep from grinning to himself. He thought Mr. Box had been a little obvious about that. Was he really expecting Jed to steal the key and open the door?

"Hmph," sniffed Jed, "it's not likely I'd forget the cheese and ham and bread I got here tonight—the first square meal I've had since I got to Boston. He can test me all he wants and I won't care. Little he knows of Silas Clark's whip or he'd not bother."

He drowsily closed his eyes. A moment later he was asleep.

3

❧ In the morning, after an hour's work at his press, Mr. Box went out. "I'll be back in an hour," he called over his shoulder.

Jed went on sweeping, but it was not long before the pile of printed handbills caught his eye. He leaned on his broom and looked at them admiringly. It was not true that he could read only his own name. Years ago his mother had taught him a few words— not many, but a few—and he had never forgotten them. He knew *boy* and *cat* and *God* and *sir.* . . . His eyes ran hungrily over the handbill, but it contained none of these words. All he could make out was the date, November, 1774.

The bells jangled as the door opened. A man in a black greatcoat walked in, closed the door and frowned at Jed. He was a giant of a man with a face carved out of rock: a great jutting chin, a long bony nose and thick brows. His eyes were small and almost disappeared into his frown.

"Mr. Box has gone out," explained Jed. "He'll be back in an hour."

"Well, well, well," said the man, looking him over. "So Titherming Box has gotten himself an apprentice now?"

"Yes, sir, I guess so," said Jed. Much to his surprise the man did not leave. He walked closer. "Are you going to wait for him?" asked Jed.

The stranger laughed. "No, no; my business can be done with you, I think. What's your name, boy?"

"Jed, sir."

"Ah." The stranger leaned against the table and looked down at him with narrowed eyes. "I don't imagine a boy like you earns many pieces of silver, eh? How'd you like to make a few shillings?"

"Oh, yes sir," said Jed eagerly. "You want something done?"

"In a manner of speaking." The man walked to the window and peered out through the glass. Then he came so close to Jed that Jed could see the old scars of smallpox on his cheeks and the hairs that grew out of his nose. "I want a little information, that's all. Not so bad, eh, boy?"

"Information?" repeated Jed in surprise.

"Aye, just a little information if you please. About Mr. Box."

"Mr. Box?" said Jed with a sinking heart.

"Where he goes. Who comes here. Who talks to him. What do you say to that, Jed?"

Jed felt a wave of anger rise in him. "No, sir," he said with a lift of his chin. "If that's what you want, then you'd better get out of here before Mr. Box comes back. I'll do you the kindness of forgetting what you've said, but if you ever come back I'll tell Mr. Box, I promise you."

The man scowled. "Come now, boy, what's he to you?"

Jed picked up his broom and held it threateningly. "Never you mind," he said flatly. "Just get out."

With a shrug the man went to the door. "If you change your mind just ask for Hovey at the Gray Horse Tavern."

"I won't," called Jed indignantly.

"Little fool," said the man and slammed the door behind him.

"And who was that?" asked Mr. Box, entering just as the stranger hurried away down the street.

Jed hesitated. Mr. Box *seemed* kind. The two loaves of bread that Jed had baked that morning had come from the oven black as chimney dirt, but Mr. Box had neither whipped him nor scolded him for it. He'd only said mildly, "How very interesting!"

But Jed was not used to kindness. He decided it

was safer to keep this to himself. He said in a clear voice, "The man wanted business with you, but he couldn't wait."

"Ah, then he'll be back, I'm sure," said Mr. Box cheerfully, and went upstairs.

When Jed had first come to Boston two years ago the harbor had been full of ships: galleons, four-masters, shallops, pinks and ketches. Now the harbor was nearly as empty and quiet as a millpond, the only ship in sight a British man-of-war that guarded the harbor night and day. From what Jed had heard at the smithy this was because England was angry with the people in Boston town. Jed wasn't sure what was wrong, but he did know it was a serious business for Boston to be punished this way. Boston depended upon the sea for its life. It was attached to the land by only one marshy, bumpy road that was sometimes covered by water. Now ships were turned away and had to sail on to Salem or Marblehead or Gloucester instead. It meant that food and hemp and paper and clothes were hard to come by in Boston. This was why people had done so much grumbling when they stopped at Silas Clark's smithy, and this was why the red-coated soldiers were living in town now.

But for Jed it meant only that he had a nearly empty harbor to gaze upon when he went for a walk. Such freedom was new to him, but it seemed that Mr. Box believed in fresh air. "You've tidied the kitchen? Swept the shop? Salted the meat?" he would say.

"Well, then, get a little fresh air before bedtime. Go on—off with you, now."

Jed would run off down the street, excited at being free for an hour. He would skip along the cobbles, dodging horses and people, until he reached the wharves. There he would sit on a pile of rope and watch the gulls swooping down from the sky for food. He would stare at the dull, gray water and think about his new master.

He wasn't accustomed to thinking. There had been little time for it in his life so far. Now he found himself wondering over and over again why he had refused silver from that man Hovey. Some evenings he decided he was just a plain fool. He'd never in his whole life owned so much as a shilling—what a sound two of them would make jingling in his pocket! And he owed nothing to Mr. Box; not really. Ever since his mother had died he'd been passed from one man to another. He'd learned to be tough and look out for himself. Nobody had ever done him a favor or a good turn, and here he had turned down money for spying on Mr. Box—real money! He turned this thought over and over in his mind, wondering at himself. It was like meeting Jed Crane for the first time as a person. It made him curious as to who and what he was.

Tonight, seeing the first star of the evening blink at him, Jed stood up with a sigh. It was quiet here, but it was time to go back and light the lantern for Mr. Box, and so he said goodbye to the harbor.

There was the feel of new snow in the air and Jed quickened his steps, thinking of the embers left in the kitchen hearth. As soon as he reached the shop he'd blow them into a flame and warm his fingers over them.

As he turned up Milk Street and passed a dark alley, something shot out from the wall to trip him. Before he fell flat across the cobblestones a hand reached out and pulled him into the blackness of the alley. A voice he had heard once before said grimly, "All right, boy, it's time you 'n me had another talk."

It was the man called Hovey. Jed gaped at him in surprise.

"I've been waiting for you to come and see me," said Hovey. "Seeing as how you haven't, I thought I'd do a mite of persuading." Arms encircled Jed, and before he could cry out he was twisted around so that Hovey's elbow pushed at his windpipe. He could hardly breathe.

"I warned you," said Hovey savagely. "And I'm a man who gets his way. I want the key to that room. I want news of Box's friends. I want lots of things."

Jed kicked him hard in the shins.

"Young ruffian. I warn you, another kick and I'll——"

Jed pried one hand loose and pushed at Hovey's elbow. He dislodged it just enough to draw a deep breath. Once he could breathe again, he bit Hovey's wrist as hard as he could. The man gave a howl of

pain, and Jed squirmed free. "No," he shouted back at Hovey. "Never, never, never!"

He ran out of the alley and up the street. Lights were being lit here and there in houses, and Jed ducked to avoid being seen. At last he slid into a dark lane and stopped, panting, to catch new breath. There were tears in his eyes, but they were tears of anger as much as of hurt. He was going to have to tell Mr. Box now about Hovey. . . . Aye, he must spill out the whole story so the man would know he had an enemy. But he didn't want to, for would Mr. Box believe him? Wouldn't Mr. Box decide it was safer not to have a boy in the shop at all? Then he would send him back to Silas Clark's smithy or to someone just as bad, and the unfairness of it made Jed furious. Mr. Box would surely never believe he'd told Hovey nothing. He'd no sooner found a good place than somebody had to spoil it for him. He hated Hovey with all his heart.

After a while he walked slowly toward Water Street and the shop. The bells jangled as he opened and closed the door. From upstairs Mr. Box called, "That you, Jed?"

"Yes, sir," said Jed miserably.

"Lock the door and come upstairs, please."

Jed obeyed, climbed the stairs and opened the door to Mr. Box's bedroom. The room was in shadow except for a candle that burned at a small table. It outlined the shape of a bed and a desk and shone full on the faces of the two men who sat at the table. One man was Mr. Box. The other was Hovey.

"What's the matter, Jed?" asked Mr. Box in a kindly voice. "You look as if you're seeing a ghost. This is a friend of mine, Hovey Parker."

"Oh—oh no, sir!" gasped Jed. "He's no friend of yours, Mr. Box—truly he isn't. Why, he nearly killed me a few minutes ago. He wants me to spy on you!"

Mr. Box smiled. "Nearly killed you?" He shook his head at Hovey. "I told you to be gentle, Hovey —shame on you." His eyes were twinkling as he turned to Jed. "I fear, my boy, that Hovey was only acting on my orders."

"Orders?" repeated Jed dumbly.

Mr. Box stood up and held out the key to the forbidden room. "You've passed your tests very nicely this first week, Jed. You've done better work than you realized. I think it's time to show you now what your real work will be. Do you by chance know what counterfeiting is . . . ?"

4

❦ "Counterfeiting?" echoed Jed. He shook his head.

Mr. Box picked up the candle, making the shadows jump, and led the way to the door of the secret room. "Dear, dear," he said with a twinkle. "Hovey, we really must teach this boy something of the world." Opening the door, he walked in. He beckoned to Jed, saying, "Come and tell me what you see, my boy."

Jed looked into the room and was disappointed. "It's just like the room downstairs," he said. "It's a printing shop."

"Ah, but a shop that nobody must know about," said Mr. Box. "You see, Jed, I print money here."

THE *Bells* OF *Freedom* 33

Jed looked at him in astonishment. "Lor," he gasped. "Truly?"

Mr. Box smiled. "Well, not truly, Jed. I make false money."

Jed's eyes were huge. "What's the good of it, then?"

Hovey laughed, showing big yellow teeth. "There's plenty good to it, boy. Mr. Box makes such fine money nobody sees that it's false. He's a rare one, he is—a proper artist. And if false money buys meat and drink and clothes, what's the difference to it?"

"It does all that?" asked Jed in amazement.

"Aye. You could go out tonight and spend an eight-pound note right here in Boston."

"No," said Mr. Box sharply. "Not in Boston. Never in Boston, Hovey. It's why you and I have never been to jail—and don't you forget it."

"I was only funning the boy," said Hovey.

Mr. Box turned to Jed. "Perhaps you wondered why I chose you—why I took you from Silas Clark?"

Since he had wondered very much, Jed nodded.

Mr. Box tapped his brow with a finger. "Brains, Jed. Something Silas Clark would never recognize. You have intelligence—I could see it in your face. You're loyal, too. So much the better. Both Hovey and I have need of a good boy, eh, Hovey?"

So it was to be his brains he was to use with Mr. Box. The idea pleased Jed. "What am I to do?" he asked.

"Why, deliver my false money to friends of mine outside of Boston town. The authorities are getting suspicious. The last package was caught—Hovey was carrying it and got away in the dark, but it was a shock to us. Until then we'd walked in and out of Boston town as boldly as any other men of business. But it's not likely they'll suspect a boy."

"No, sir. When do I start?" asked Jed eagerly.

"Not for a while," said Mr. Box. "You'd be in a pretty mess if I let you go too soon. You'd not even be able to get to Roxbury without knowing how to read signposts or a map."

"Oh, but I could ask," Jed promised him.

Mr. Box laughed sharply. "Yes, you could ask —ask a dozen people, and every one of 'em would remember the boy who asked questions. Oh, no. First we must teach you how to read."

"Read?" gasped Jed.

"Yes. Signs, maps, directions."

Jed drew in his breath sharply at the thought—to think that he was going to be taught how to read! The very idea dazzled him. He had longed for years to learn. Now Mr. Box had taken him in, given him work he could do easily and food to fill his stomach, and he was going to teach him to read as well. Jed said fervently, "Mr. Box—Mr. Box, I'll be the best errand boy you've ever had. I'll do anything. And I already know seven words besides my own name. How long do you think it will be before I can read books?"

Mr. Box smiled. "Not long for such a bright

boy, Jed. In fact we'll go downstairs now and have our first lesson. Fetch candles, Hovey—a hornbook, a primer and a map."

In this manner Jed began his first lessons in reading. He had never seen a New England Primer before and he spent every spare minute looking at the old one that Mr. Box owned. He loved the woodcuts in it, and very quickly he began to learn the words. He loved turning over the rhymes in his head: "In Adam's fall we sinned all." "The cat does play, and after slay." "Time cuts down all, both great and small."

Now when Jed walked to the market every morning to buy food there were many more things for him to enjoy, for Boston was full of signs. Once he had admired only their bright pictures; now he could read the words under them. There was one sign he had passed every day that bore the picture of a tree, a bird, a ship and a mug of steaming cider. He thought he would never forget the moment when he puzzled out the rhyme that went with them. He stood with his head thrown back and read:

> *This is the tree that never grew,*
> *This is the bird that never flew,*
> *This is the ship that never sailed,*
> *This is the mug that never failed.*

With a grin he turned away, but the next day he came back to read it all over again.

He learned the names of the streets, too, for when he had worked for Silas Clark he had seen almost nothing of Boston. Now he was free to roam as he pleased, and he explored until he knew the town by heart. Because it was surrounded by water on three sides he couldn't get lost for long. On the fourth side of it was the Town Gate and the road across the marshes to Roxbury, but Jed went only once through the gates to stare at the gallows and that was enough.

Going to market every morning, he began to notice now that there was a great deal going on in Boston. Every day brought changes. He noticed it especially when he bought food. He didn't expect to find more than a few wormy apples in November, but now there were no longer limes or pimentos or coffee from the West Indies, either. Soon it was impossible to buy a saddle of mutton for Mr. Box, or beef of any kind, and nearly every day they had to eat fish.

"Why?" he asked of Mr. Box. "Why have the English closed up the harbor so nobody can bring us food by sea? Why are they angry at Boston?"

Mr. Box shrugged. "England doesn't like the way Boston behaves, that's all. She's punishing the town."

"But why?"

"Ask a lot of questions, don't you, boy? Well, the colonies belong to England—right?"

"Right," said Jed.

"And so England makes the rules. She sits an

ocean away from us and decides what people here should do and not do. Some of the rules make sense and some don't. The people in Boston have been ignoring the ones that don't."

"Oh," said Jed, frowning over this.

"So last year the King decided to get tough. He sent General Gage over to be governor of Massachusetts, and this general decided Boston should be taught a lesson. He closed up the harbor and asked for eleven regiments of soldiers to show who's boss. That's when the redcoats came. And Boston town will slowly starve if she doesn't knuckle under."

"And will she?" asked Jed eagerly.

Mr. Box shrugged. "Who knows? She hasn't yet. It's none of my business, and none of yours, but people here are stubborn and there are some who say there'll be fighting."

"Really?" gasped Jed. He wondered if Mr. Box meant a war. There had already been fights in the street between red-coated soldiers and Boston men. He knew that British soldiers drilled every day in the Common. He decided he would keep his eyes open for the right and the wrong of it. He found that it was fun to be using his brains after two years of hard, dull, mindless work.

Now, free of the noise of Silas Clark's smithy, Jed's days were quiet. There was no longer the pounding of iron against iron as Silas Clark's anvil shaped hot metal. Jed no longer heard the sizzle of heat meeting cold as the nails or horseshoes were plunged into water for quick cooling. There was no longer the smell of steam and fire and sweat and horses. Since there was very little business going on in Boston now—and Mr. Box never looked for more —few men came to the print shop. Mr. Box did not mind. If he was not printing bills of fare or handbills downstairs he was printing false money upstairs.

"What shall it be tonight, m'boy?" he would ask merrily. "A Rhode Island twenty-shilling bill or a forty-shilling New Hampshire bill?"

He would build up the fire and light the betty lamps and rub ink on the copper plate and print one sheet of bills after another at his press, letting Jed hang them up to dry. He was a painstaking counterfeiter; the bills that did not measure up he burned in the fire. When he had a little pile of good false bills Mr. Box would sit down with ink and pen and carefully copy the signatures of the men who had signed the bills. Jed could see that he was a real artist. The finished bills he tucked away in a small leather bag for Jed to deliver one day to friends.

And every night he would take out the map and say, "All right, m'boy, it's practice time. Show me how to go to Medford."

From the north of Boston Jed would trace the lines on the map with one finger. Down Fish and Anne Streets, across the drawbridge into Boston proper. Out over the High Street and through the gates. Past the gallows and across the flats and up the country high road to Medford.

"Well done," Mr. Box would say. "But for what reason would you be leaving Boston? Remember, you might be questioned at the town gate."

Jed would think a moment. "I'd be going into the country for food. No—this is December. . . . Not food. I'd be going for birch kindling for the kitchen fire."

Mr. Box would nod. "But mind you take the time to bring back a basketful of bark or twigs."

Soon, however, Mr. Box came home furious, to report that things were growing tighter in Boston. Now, in order to leave town, a person had to go first to Province House and get a pass from the army. "That infernal General Gage," he exploded. "It isn't enough that nobody can get into town by sea. Now he must know who leaves by the gates, and why."

"I wouldn't be able to use kindling as a reason any more?" asked Jed sadly.

"Well, there are more ways to leave town than by the gate," said Mr. Box mysteriously. "Pah! Tied up like a sack, that's what we are, and hungry as well. Only cheering part of it," he added gloomily, "is that the redcoats and General Gage are just as hungry."

But if there was less food, if sometimes there was only bread for supper, Jed scarcely minded. He was warm, he was happy, he was well treated for the first time in his life—and he was learning to read. What more could he ask?

5

Carefully and silently Jed spelled out the words on the sign that had been nailed to the tree. "Strike for freedom! Down with Oppression!" He had a little trouble with the word *oppression* but finally spelled it out. "Citizens of Massachusetts, the time has come to fight for your rights!"

"So you know how to read," said a voice beside him.

Jed looked up to see a boy of thirteen or fourteen watching him. "Aye," he admitted.

The boy pointed to the poster. "What d'ye make of that?"

Jed said cautiously, "I don't know." The boy had the brightest yellow hair he'd ever seen, and freckles all over his face. He looked as if he'd be fun to know, but it wasn't just shyness that made Jed hesitate. He knew by now that only half of the people in Boston would be happy to read the words on this sign. They were called rebels because they were ready to fight for their rights. The other half of the people shuddered at such a thought. They wanted to see this quarrel with the King settled peacefully, even if it took years. They were known as Tories.

"It's just a sign," Jed said at last, deciding to say nothing.

"Aye—and here come the redcoats to tear it down," gasped the boy. "Quick, run down the alley."

The two of them took to their heels and ended up a street away, panting for breath. "Those redcoats!" said the boy scornfully. "One of these days they'll be gone—and not just to Roxbury, either! Ben Wheeler's my name. What's yours?"

"Jed Crane." He hesitated and then said, "Do you think there'll be fighting someday?"

"Of course," said Ben. "You been out of Boston lately?"

Jed shook his head.

"Well, while the redcoats are drilling every day on the Common here, the people are drilling in every town outside of Boston. There's bound to be a fight.

People are *mad*." He stared at Jed suspiciously. "You a Tory?"

"Me?" Jed was surprised. "I don't know. I'm not on anybody's side."

"You're not? You mean you don't care?"

Jed shook his head. "It's enough for me to have food and a roof over my head. What's it to me if there's fighting?"

Ben looked at him in astonishment. "But this is your country—you live here! Don't you care about freedom?"

"Freedom?" echoed Jed in surprise.

"Are you that fond of jumping when King George cracks his whip?" Ben demanded, and with one last scornful glance he walked away from Jed.

Jed was thoughtful as he walked back to the shop. He was learning to read, he was fed well and Mr. Box had given him a warm woolen jacket for winter. And yet—and yet, were any of these things of more value than freedom? Once he had been dragged aboard a ship like a sack of potatoes and made to work for a captain who cared nothing about him. That captain had sold him to Silas Clark for twenty pounds. Silas Clark might as well have kept him in chains for all the freedom Jed had known. It had been *Do this, Do that*, and nothing Jed could do about it. Oh yes, he knew very well the value of freedom. It was the most precious thing in the world.

Was it like this with the people in Boston town, and in Massachusetts? Were they trying to win free-

dom from a harsh master? Was this King a cruel one
for them?

"Tell me more," he begged of Mr. Box that
evening as they sat down to a dinner of boiled fish
again.

Mr. Box looked at him long and hard. "Jed," he
said, "keep your nose out of it. It's of no concern to
you or me."

"But will the people here have a chance if it
comes to fighting?" he asked stubbornly.

Mr. Box shrugged. "If there's fighting, Jed, the
better side will win. And whoever wins—well, that's
the side I'll be on. That's where the money will lie;
and money," he said, waving his fork at Jed, "is
what buys life. It's what keeps body and soul together, and don't you forget it, m'boy."

It occurred to Jed for the first time that Mr.
Box had never been bound out to Silas Clark. It made
for a difference between them.

Jed made his first trip out of Boston in February, when the ground was white with snow. He did
not go by the town gate. Hovey smuggled him out
by boat.

"You'd never make it through the gates," said
Mr. Box as he tied the counterfeit bills into small
bundles. "You might get a pass if you said you were
bringing back wood or food for the redcoats—but
I doubt they'd give such a pass to a boy," he added
dryly. "Or you could pretend to go fishing, but

then you'd have to bring back some fish. Ever been
fishing, Jed?"

Jed wordlessly shook his head.

"It leaves us no choice. Hovey has a boat hidden by the river, and the river's not frozen over yet
this winter. You've got more meat on your bones
now than when I first saw you—you can row your
way out of town."

"Where do I deliver the money?" asked Jed.

"Show him, Hovey," said Mr. Box.

Hovey brought out the map and they leaned
over it. "To Cambridge, across the Charles River,"
he said. "You'll leave in an hour. It's about a mile
across, and a dark night—you can hide the boat on
the opposite shore. Then you'll walk around Cambridge—like this—until you meet the road to Menotomy. There's a house here," he said, marking the
map with an X. "It stands on the right side of the
road, with a well sweep in the front yard, and an old
apple tree that leans to the south. You'll knock, ask
for a Mr. Dustin and deliver the money to him.
When you've delivered it you'll walk to the river
and row back to Boston."

Jed thought a moment. "But if it's dark when I
row back, how will I know where to land?"

"I'll be waiting for you," said Hovey. "I'll have
the lantern. I'll shine it for half a minute every fifteen minutes after midnight. Only a crack will show,
but you'll see it from the water."

"Think you can do this?" asked Mr. Box. Looking Jed full in the face he said sternly, "It's two months' work you're carrying. You won't be careless?"

"Oh no," gasped Jed, excited at proving himself at last. He would be fearless and brave and trustworthy—he hoped. Getting caught would be a wretched way to repay Mr. Box for his kindness. He only wished that he need not go and come in the dark.

Mr. Box reached out to rough up his hair affectionately. "You've learned well, m'boy. Not enough to make the bills yet, but that day will come. We'll make a good little counterfeiter out of you, eh, Hovey? Now I've put the money into this belt—hold still while I buckle it around your middle."

"Yes, sir."

"And talk to no one. There may be spies out tonight—spies for the rebels and spies for the English. Be careful."

"Yes, sir."

With the belt under Jed's clothes they went downstairs to the print shop where few customers came these days. The light shone on dusty handbills and plates of copper, and on the wooden bench where Jed slept. As he and Hovey passed through the door into the darkness Jed looked back at Mr. Box standing in his shop. The light shone full on his round, kindly face. Jed realized it would be a long night for Mr. Box.

With Hovey guiding him they made their way

through the dark alleys like two shadows. It was
past nine, and no one belonged on the streets but the
Town Watch, but there was little danger from them.
The Watch made enough noise and carried enough
light with them to be seen and heard from a distance.

The smell of the river grew stronger as they
reached the Common. Here they ducked from tree
to tree and ran across the cleared spaces until they
came to the river. "Out here," whispered Hovey,
tugging at his arm, and they tiptoed over the splin-
tered boards of an old dock. Water slapped gently
against its sides. At the very end of it Hovey lay
down and felt beneath it. He pressed a rope into
Jed's hand. "The boat lies below. I'll pull it from
under the dock and you jump in. The oars lie on
the floor."

A moment later Jed was seated at the oars.

"There's a ship's compass in your pocket,"
Hovey reminded him. "And a lantern to read it by
—shine it no more than a second and only if you
lose your way."

But Mr. Box had chosen his time well. There
was only a sliver of moon that shed no light, but it
was a crisp, clear night with stars scattered across the
sky. Jed could soon make out the thick trees that
divided the Charles and the Mystic Rivers. He
headed west, rowing soundlessly and feeling lonelier
than he had ever felt in his life. But he was sure he
would not get lost: he had learned to read from both
the primer and from Mr. Box's maps and he already

knew the shape and size of Cambridge. By closing his eyes he could recall every road and landmark he must look for.

The boat struck land and Jed jumped out and stood a moment in the darkness to get his bearings. It was cold here by the water and he stood in icy, wet mud. He had landed in a jungle of cattails, and they rustled behind and around him like ghosts. With a shiver he drew out the oars and laid them in the bottom of the boat. Then he pulled the boat deep among the grasses to hide it, brushed away the cattails and began to walk.

He had taken only a few steps when a hand shot out of the darkness. A man's voice said harshly, "Tell us who you are and where you come from, and be quick about it."

Jed gasped. His teeth began to chatter from terror as well as cold, and he found he couldn't speak. He knew he ought to try and run away, but the hand on his shoulder was like iron and his feet were mired in mud. He wriggled a little and then was still.

"Well?" demanded the voice sharply.

To Jed's despair a second voice said, "I swear he came from Boston."

"Aye, and in a boat. A rowboat. Shine the lantern on his face and let's see what kind of fish we've caught."

A sliver of light escaped from a lantern and

then was covered over quickly. "It's only a boy," said the voice in surprise.

"Take him up to the house and see what you can get from him. I'll stay—it may be that Hitchborne will still come."

House, thought Jed. If it was a house, then perhaps they were not redcoats after all. The hand on his shoulder fell to his back and he was pushed, not ungently, through the grass to a rough road. Now he could see three men silhouetted against the sky, and he tried to think of what story to tell them. He was so numb from cold and worry that he could think of nothing to say. He wondered if these men would notice his bulging waist and guess he wore a belt of money. He began to wonder if he had failed Mr. Box.

Up ahead he saw the black shape of a house, small and low to the ground. He stumbled over stones and nearly fell. A door opened, showing light behind it. The three men picked up Jed and swiftly set him inside before the door closed on the night.

6

❧ "Well, well, and what have we here?" asked a man standing in front of the bright fire on the hearth.

It was a small room with stone walls and tamped-down floor of earth—one of the old houses, guessed Jed, built years and years ago when people were new to the country. The hearth was tall, with a rough, plank mantel. The man standing with one arm along that mantel was tall, too, with a head of hair as red as ginger. But he did not look unkind, nor did he wear a British uniform. Jed gave a sigh of relief.

"And who did you think we might be?" asked

the red-haired man, noticing his relief. To the other three he said, "It's all right. One boy I can certainly handle alone. No, Tim—you stay. I may have need of you." As the others left, the red-haired man said cheerfully, "Well?"

"I—I thought you might be British soldiers," whispered Jed. "Are you?"

The man did not say. Instead he asked. "And what would the redcoats do to you?"

"Why—put me in jail. For leaving Boston town without their leave, I suppose."

"Sit down, lad," he said. "Tim, draw a cup of hot tea for us. The boy looks blue with cold. And just why have you left Boston without leave, lad?"

In spite of himself Jed trusted the man. There was nothing fancy about him. He wore plain homespun, his face was brown from the sun and he had a friendly, cheerful manner. He said, "Because there's no other way to leave Boston town."

The man grinned. "This lad knows how to keep from answering questions, Tim. A neat trick." To Jed he said, "Here's your tea, lad. Drink up."

"What question did you want me to answer?" asked Jed cautiously, and put his lips to the mug. The tea tasted bitter but it warmed him.

The man's bright eyes were watching him. "Let's start again. You can tell me which side you're on, for one thing."

Jed realized they thought he was a spy. On this matter he could be frank at least. "I'm on nobody's

side," he said bluntly. "Do I have to be? I'm only on an errand for my master."

"Well, then, which side is your master on? Is he Tory or rebel?"

Jed thought about this. "I asked him once. He said I must keep my nose out of it. He said there might be fighting sometime. He said the better side would win and that was the side he'd be on."

The man's face darkened. "I see—one of *them*. And you—do you feel this way, too? Speak up, lad. You've been captured, you know. You've little to lose from speaking the truth."

"I don't know," said Jed. "Except—except I've never liked being pushed around. I met a boy once who said that's what the King is doing to people over here. If that's the case," he said frankly, "then I lean a little to the rebel side."

"Even if I'm a British redcoat?" asked the man.

Jed said recklessly, "Yes, even if you're a redcoat."

The man chuckled. "But you'd rather not take sides at all, is that it?"

Jed nodded.

"Then," said the man quickly, "what's your errand here in the dead of the night?"

He had him there. Jed decided to tell half of the truth. "I'm carrying money for my master," he said, and thinking fast added, "It's a—a debt that must be paid quickly. Yes, and secretly, too, so my master sent me with it." He lifted his chin defiantly. "It's

in a belt around my middle, if you want to know. I
suppose you'll take it from me now and Mr. Box
will punish me, and he's the kindest master I've had."

"Box?" repeated the man.

"Titherming Box of Water Street, printer."

The redhead nodded. "Tim, is there such a
man? You know Water Street."

Tim nodded. "Aye, there is. I've seen his sign
but never the man."

"Tory?"

"Not to my knowledge. He's on none of the
lists."

The redhead nodded. "Very well, lad, you've
treated us frankly. I believe you." He thought a
moment. "We have need of someone to deliver a
message in Boston town tomorrow. Perhaps if we
let you go you'll return the favor by taking it back
with you?"

"I might," said Jed cautiously. "Who is it to?"

"Come back and find out," the redhead told
him, getting to his feet. "How far do you go tonight?"

"To a house on the road to Menotomy."

He nodded. "Tim, take the lad to the Menotomy road. If he has nothing to hide he'll not mind
the company." He stuck out his hand. "I'll see you
again. What's your name?"

"Jed Crane."

"All right, Jed, be gone with you. Tim will
bring you back."

THE Bells OF Freedom   55

Jed could hardly believe his ears. He decided that with so much that was political going on—between the King and the people here, and between the army and the militia—nobody had any interest at all in counterfeiters. But he couldn't relax yet. He still had Mr. Dustin to meet.

Tim did not take him through Cambridge. "Too many dogs," he whispered. He took him past the town by way of fields and marshes. When they got back to the Menotomy road Cambridge lay behind them and Jed was wet to the knees from snow and marsh mud.

Jed told the man about the bent apple tree and the well sweep and Tim nodded. "I know the house. It lies just beyond the next turn in the road. I'll wait for you here."

Jed glanced at him in surprise. "You trust me?"

Tim laughed. "The Captain does, and that's good enough for me. Don't worry, though; I'll be keeping my eye on you. There are no redcoats here to help you if you should be up to something."

"So you're not redcoats or Tories," Jed told him triumphantly. "You're rebels, both of you!"

Tim only grinned, his teeth showing white in the dark. "Go along with you now. Me and my big mouth."

Jed left him and walked up to the house with the twisted apple tree that showed black against the deep-blue night sky. A dog began barking. When Jed knocked, a candle showed through the seams of the door. Presently the door opened an inch. "Who is it?"

"I was told I could find Mr. Dustin here, sir."

The door was opened. A gruff voice said, "Very well, come in. He's here, and who might you be?"

"A friend."

By the light of the candle Jed saw a stout man in a nightshirt and white wig. "Are you Mr. Dustin? Mr. Box sent me."

"Well, about time, too," gasped the man. "You have something for me? Give it over quickly, boy, before the master of the house comes down. I'm only a guest here."

Jed pulled off his belt of money and handed it to him. "I was to get something from you, too, sir," he reminded the man.

"Yes, yes, of course. It's right here." By the light of the candle the man drew a belt from his own waist. It was just like the one Jed had given him except that it carried real money, in payment for the counterfeit bills. "There you are," whispered the man. "Now hurry. Tell Box the next delivery goes to Marshall. You understand? Marshall."

Jed nodded. He was practically pushed from the door and the door shut behind him. A voice from above called out, "And who was that, Mr. Dustin? Was someone at the door?"

Jed turned and hurried down the road. In the shadows he found Tim again, and was taken back to the house near the river. Fifteen minutes later he was being led to the boat, with his red-haired friend showing him the way.

"You have at least two hours until dawn," he told Jed. "And I'm very glad to have met you, lad. We may have need of a boy like you someday."

"I don't even know your name," pointed out Jed.

"And won't," said the man. "These days it's safer not to know—but if ever I have need of you I'll know where to find you, and I'll call myself the Red-Haired Captain."

"The red-haired captain," repeated Jed. "All right. But I don't know what need you'd have of me, sir—although of course I'd enjoy very much meeting you again," he added quickly.

The captain chuckled. "We can always use a lad who leans a little to the rebel side. Mind you keep leaning a little, Jed."

Jed smiled, but he did not plan to take any sides. Mr. Box had told him not to and he had every intention of obeying his master. It was exciting enough to be errand boy for Mr. Box in the middle of the night and also, very briefly, an errand boy by day for the red-haired captain.

"Here's the slip of paper with the message," said the captain, crumpling paper into his hand. "You remember to whom you take it?"

Jed nodded. "Aye—to Master Paul Revere, the silversmith, on Clark's Wharf."

"Good. I trust you on it, too—don't forget."

Jed slid into the boat and picked up the oars, the captain gave the boat a shove and Jed was off again to Boston. It had been a long night, but it was coming to an end at last. Now that he was on his way home he could forget his terror and remember what fun it had been to have an adventure all by himself. He thought he might tell Mr. Box about meeting the captain but not about the message he was to deliver to Mr. Revere. Then he decided he'd better not tell Mr. Box anything at all.

It was not long before he saw a sliver of light from the dock on the west shore. It disappeared. A few minutes later it shone again. When Jed rowed up to the dock Hovey was waiting. Seeing Jed, he heaved a great sigh of relief.

"You made it," he said, and shook his head. "What took you so long? You've got the money?"

Jed leaped onto the dock, took off the belt of money and handed it to Hovey.

"Praise be," said Hovey. "We'll have need of this to buy food and ink." He reached out and patted Jed on the head. "You've done well tonight, boy," he said, and his voice was gentler than Jed had heard it before. "Now let's slip back and tell Mr. Box you're safe. He must be near out of his mind from worry by this hour."

7

❧ The next morning on his way to market Jed
crossed the drawbridge into North Boston and cut
down Fish Street until he reached Clark's Wharf. It
was a beautiful morning, with the sun dancing on the
ice-blue water of the harbor. Clark's Wharf reached
out toward the sea like a long, blunt finger. Jed had
seen it once before, two summers ago, when boys had
stripped and dived into the water from the wharf.
. . . He had stood and envied them. That year it had
been one of the busiest corners of Boston, with sailors
in stocking caps and earrings, and ships' mates bel-
lowing orders over boxes of cargo. The warehouses
and sail lofts were deserted now. The only men in

sight were townspeople repairing the stout planks of the wharf. The selectmen had put them to work so they wouldn't go hungry. With the harbor closed and guarded by the British there was nothing else for them to do.

Jed walked along the wharf peering into the shops that lined one side of it. He soon found Mr. Revere's, and as he entered the shop he heard the familiar pounding of a hammer against an anvil. A man stood in front of a brick furnace. As Jed watched, the man turned back to the crimping block, gave a few blows with a hammer to the silver pitcher he held, and set it down to cool.

"There, Betty," he said to the girl waiting in the corner. "Mended as good as new. No need to cry over it—now, was there?"

"Oh indeed there was," gasped the girl, wiping red eyes with her apron. "For if the missus knew I'd melted off the handle—oh dear, but it would have gone badly with me. 'Tis her very best pitcher."

"And still is," said the man. He had a pleasant face, with a square jaw and soft brown eyes. His mouth was wide and straight and tucked in at the corners as if he smiled more often than he frowned. Seeing Jed, he said, "And what may I do for you, lad?"

The serving-girl plucked at his sleeve. "I'll be leaving now, Master Revere. How much do I owe you? I've my wages right here."

Mr. Revere gave a careless wave of his hand. 'Never you mind, Betty—keep your wages."

The girl brightened. "Oh, thank ye—thank ye kindly, sir," she said, dropping a curtsy. "Oh, but I'm beholden to you. Thank you again, sir." She flew out of the shop with the pitcher wrapped in her apron.

"I've a message for you," Jed said shyly. "It was given me in Cambridge last night."

The man lifted his brows. "Oh?"

Jed handed it to him. It was not sealed. Mr. Revere read it and smiled faintly.

"Thank you," he said, lifting his warm brown eyes to Jed. His smile deepened. "And have you read it, too?"

Jed flushed. "Yes, sir. I mean—I've only lately learned to read. I try myself on everything."

"And what did it say?"

"It said, 'Joseph is safe.' "

Mr. Revere nodded. "You read very well," he said dryly, "and you've brought me good news of a friend. What's your name, lad?"

"Jed Crane. Apprenticed to Mr. Box, printer and engraver on Water Street, sir."

"Ah—an engraver, eh? That makes him a competitor of mine. I don't believe I've met the man."

Jed wondered if he should have mentioned Mr. Box. He turned to go, and then he stopped in astonishment. "If you're an engraver, too," he said eagerly, "are you the same Mr. Revere who engraved the print of the Boston Massacre?"

Mr. Revere nodded. "But that was several years ago, you know."

Jed grinned. "Oh yes, sir, but it was corking good. I've seen that one, all right. It used to hang in Mr. Clark's smithy."

Smiling, Mr. Revere walked with him to the door. "I'm glad you liked it," he said. "Thank you for bringing the note."

What adventures he was having, Jed thought as he walked into the sunshine again—and all because Mr. Box had bought his services from Silas Clark. Imagine meeting the man who had made that fine print of the Boston Massacre, with all those redcoats lined up and their muskets going off in puffs of smoke, and men falling down all over the place. Mr. Box was an artist, and an engraver, too. He wished Mr. Box would make a print like that. Jed was sure he could do anything he chose to do, and it must be dull work copying money all the time.

He asked Mr. Box about it that night.

"Dull?" said Mr. Box in astonishment. "Dull work counterfeiting money?" They were upstairs in the secret shop. A cold February wind had sprung up from the sea to rattle the glass in the windows, but it was cozy and warm by the fire. "Hovey, this boy knows nothing of the ways of this world," said Mr. Box with a twinkle. "My dear Jed, I make much more money copying bills than I could ever make printing pictures. What does it cost me to print counterfeit money? Only some paper, some ink, a press and my skill. I make twenty pounds worth of false money and people are delighted to pay me ten pounds to spend the bills. They make a profit; I make a profit. And that, my dear Jed, makes sense."

"Yes, sir," Jed said sadly. "It's just that a picture is good to look at and think about."

"Then one of these days I'll make a picture just for you, Jed."

"Oh, I'd like that, Mr. Box. Really?"

His master stared at him thoughtfully. He said in a dry voice, "If you were an engraver, Jed, and had to choose between making counterfeit money and a picture, which would you choose?"

"A picture, of course."

Hovey said with a growl, "It's not natural. I told you the boy's too honest for my taste, Titherming."

Mr. Box beamed at him. "A trait we must not encourage, eh, Hovey? Never mind, he's new to us still. Come closer, my boy, I'm going to begin engraving a new plate tonight—you can learn how it's done. No printing of bills for a while. I'm going to engrave a new Rhode Island bill, and from the one plate we'll print hundreds of copies."

Jed drew closer. While Hovey arranged the lamps for close work, Mr. Box took out his engraving tool and a sheet of copper. On its surface he had already traced the scrollwork and lettering of the Rhode Island bill. With his tool he began, carefully and delicately, to carve lines in the copper that would catch the ink when it was printed.

After half an hour Jed sat down and Mr. Box looked up with a smile. "Tired? Very well, you can read to me from the Massachusetts *Spy*. And Jed——"

"Yes, sir?"

"There will be another trip for you next week, and more after that. You're proving a real treasure to Hovey and me, m'boy."

It was the first real compliment that Mr. Box had given him, and Jed glowed under it. How kind Mr. Box was! Life had never seemed so good before.

8

❧ Spring came early this year to Boston town. Fruit trees bloomed white and pink in the Common and in the gardens of every home in town. But lovelier than the trees was the thought of the fruit that could soon be picked from their branches and the seeds that could be planted in the gardens. People in Boston had not had enough to eat since the harbor had closed.

Other colonies and towns tried to help. Virginia sent flour and money, Maryland sent bread and grain, and from Marblehead came dried codfish. The carts of food still rolled in across the Neck to Boston, past the mud flats and the gallows and the town pasture to the gates, but there was never enough to go around.

If the quarrel between the King and Boston grew worse Jed was not really aware of it. He did hear that Mr. Revere was being watched by the redcoats because of his rides to New York and Philadelphia during the winter. Several times the redcoats marched out of town to find and destroy ammunition in the towns around Boston, but these things Jed scarcely noticed in his hunt for food.

On his trips out of town he ate better, and he always tried to bring back a little something for Mr. Box and Hovey: a pigeon, a wild turkey, an egg or two. By mid-April he had made four new trips for Mr. Box. Usually Hovey rowed him in the dark of night to Charlestown or Cambridge or Dorchester. Then Hovey would leave him on the shore and row back alone. It worked out better this way. Coming back by daylight Jed would walk boldly through the town gates. Sometimes he hung on one of the carts carrying food, and once he pretended to be a Tory son looking for his father. It was much easier to get into Boston than to leave it, and nobody paid much attention to a twelve-year-old boy.

In mid-April Mr. Box decided that Jed was to deliver his false money to Bedford. It would be the longest trip of all, and he was to carry more money than ever before. "Because it may be your last trip for a while," explained Mr. Box. "I don't like the smell of things. Too many spies—spies for the Crown, spies for the rebels. One of these nights someone will see you sneaking out of Boston and arrest you as a common spy." He gave a snort of anger. "A spy, no less! It's getting so there's no time for honest counterfeiters!"

Jed looked forward to these trips now. He loved Boston, but now that nobody was allowed to leave it without permission, the town sometimes had the feel of a prison. And if the town seemed like a jail the British redcoats were the jailers. They drilled all day long in the Common, and if they weren't drilling they walked in the streets or sat in the taverns. The Tories were the only people who welcomed them, but nobody could forget they were there. People walked faster because of them, and talked in whispers on the street.

Outside of Boston it was a different world. There was enough food and nobody had to talk softly, because most of the redcoats stayed in Boston. Nobody asked Jed now which side he was on. They asked of each other, "Where will it end?" And on every common in every town the militia drilled with their muskets.

Hovey rowed Jed to Cambridge and left him there in the dark. Before looking for the road Jed took the time to walk past the little stone house where he had met the red-haired captain. There was no one there tonight. The door stood ajar and the room was empty. It looked as if no one had gone inside for years.

It was midmorning when he reached Bedford, and the sky over the town was a deep, deep blue with puffy white clouds skidding across it. Jed drew in deep breaths of the warm spring air. The willows were a delicate green in the sunshine, and it had been such a mild winter that the meadows were already plowed and ready to be sown with grain. He hated to think this might be his last trip. Perhaps Mr. Box was right. Perhaps the Americans were too stubborn in their quarrel with the King. Perhaps freedom wasn't worth all this fuss if it inconvenienced so many people—himself included. He kicked a stone and repeated to himself what Mr. Box had said. "It's getting so there's no place for counterfeiters any more!"

His orders this time were to go to Fitch's Tavern and ask for a man named Andrews. Although this was his sixth trip for Mr. Box he still knew very little about the counterfeiting ring. He had met Mr. Dustin at that house near Menotomy, but Hovey said the man really came from New Hampshire. Once he had left a wad of counterfeit bills in a barn outside of Dorchester—there had been no man there at all. Another time he had made his way to a big mansion in Malden and handed in a package of bills for a man called Mr. Humphrey—but a passerby told him that no one by the name of Humphrey lived in that house. It was all very secret and strange, but if Mr. Box enjoyed playing games it was all right with Jed.

In Bedford he found Fitch's Tavern, but Mr. Andrews wasn't there. "Fellow *was* here," said the landlord. "Said if anybody asked for him he'd be back tomorrow morning."

"Tomorrow!" gasped Jed. "Not until then?"

"That's what he said. Little fellow riding a sorrel horse?"

Jed didn't know but he nodded. "Thank you kindly," he said, and walked out.

He spent the rest of the day wandering around the farm lanes of Bedford. It was lucky for him that Mr. Box had given him coins for just such an emergency. He was able to eat a big supper at the tavern, but he decided not to sleep there as well. He chose instead to sleep out in a field under the stars. It was just as well. There seemed to be a great commotion in town all night long, with men on horseback riding in and out until dawn.

At sunrise he was back at Fitch's Tavern. The main room was so crowded with men that he dared hope one of them might be Mr. Andrews.

"No, no, he's not come in yet," snapped the landlord. "Can't you see this is the town's militia?"

A man stood on a bench and shouted, "Come on, boys, we'll take a little something and we'll have every dog of them before night." A great shout roared through the tavern room. Jed went over to a quiet corner and sat down.

A little man in black walked over and stood beside him. After studying Jed for a moment he said softly, "You were asking for Andrews, lad?"

Startled, Jed said, "Oh yes, sir. Can you tell me where to find him?"

"I might," the little man said gently, "if I knew to whom I was speaking."

"Box," said Jed, as he'd been told to say.

"Ah." The little man's eyes brightened. "Then I have something for you—and you have something for me, eh?" He grasped Jed by the arm and led him from the tavern. "Safer out here," he said. He stopped under a tree and brought out an oilskin packet.

In return Jed went behind the tree and returned a minute later with the money belt.

"Thank you," said the man, strapping it around his own waist. "Now, you forget you ever saw me, lad. And a safe journey back to you—but don't go by way of Concord, I pray you."

"Why not?" asked Jed.

Andrews stopped and turned. "Why, because British troops are heading there. They marched out of Boston last night. And those militiamen," he said, pointing to the tavern, "are headed for Concord, too."

"Oh," said Jed, wondering what that meant. The British were always marching somewhere to look for hidden muskets and lead. But Concord was out of his way, anyway, and he had no desire to go there. He planned to go back the way he had come, down through Menotomy and thence to Cambridge. And so he would have done, but just as he reached the tavern its doors opened and the minutemen spilled

out to run for their horses. Among them Jed saw
the red-haired captain.

"Captain!" he shouted, breaking into a run.
"Captain, wait!"

But he was too late. His friend from Cambridge
wheeled his horse and galloped away down the road.
Jed stood and watched the other men ride past, the
dust from their horses nearly choking him.

He was sorry the captain had not seen or heard
him, for he had a real longing to speak with him
again. The captain had been a friend, the second real
friend he had found, treating him fairly and with
kindness. Jed stood a moment thinking and then, forgetting Andrews' warning, he began to follow the
militia down the road to Concord. He was on his way
even before the dust settled. He scuffed along, still
without breakfast, but with his package of counterfeit bills safely delivered. The birds were beginning
to sing in the fields and the sun was melting away
the mist that had clung to the ground during the
night. It seemed to Jed as he walked that he could
hear bells ringing, as if to celebrate his return to
Boston.

There *were* bells ringing, he decided suddenly.
He stopped and turned toward Bedford to listen.
Yes, the church bell was ringing wildly in the town
behind him. He wondered why. A fire, perhaps? He
hastened his steps, expecting to meet the militia
around the next curve, or the next, hoping to find the
red-haired captain, too, who would smile his kind

smile and say, "Well, if it isn't my old friend Jed Crane."

But the militia appeared to have vanished from the road. He saw the spire of the church in Concord up ahead, and as he came to the edge of town he saw that the redcoats had already arrived there from Boston. There were soldiers everywhere—on the lawns under the trees and in chairs in front of the tavern. The scarlet of their uniforms was beautiful against the soft green grass of the April morning. But there was no sign of the militia.

Jed had no desire to meet redcoats—he could see enough of them in Boston—and so he ducked behind a house and crossed the fields to avoid the town. Near the North Bridge he swam the river and climbed a hill to dry out in the morning sun. He lay down with his hands behind his head and stared up at the blue morning sky. His clothes steamed in the hot sun. Feeling drowsy, he closed his eyes.

He had not slept long when a loud bang woke him up. Somewhere below him a musket roared, and the echo of it crashed back and forth among the hills. As Jed leaped to his feet another musket went off, and then another. Jed ran a few paces down the hill and stopped in horror.

He had found his militiamen at last—swarms of them. They were standing at one end of Concord's North Bridge and they were firing across the bridge at the other end.

They were shooting at British soldiers.

Jed's mouth dropped in astonishment. He couldn't believe his eyes. Never, never had Americans shot at redcoats before. Why, it was unheard of! Quarrel with them, yes, have fist-fights in the street with them, yes—but shoot at them? Never. The redcoats were the law of the land. The redcoats had been sent to the colonies to keep the people humble. The redcoats were England. They were the *King*.

And the redcoats were firing back.

"They don't know what they're doing," gasped Jed. "The militia must have gone mad. They'll be hanged for this. . . . Oh, dear God, they don't have a chance."

There were tears in his eyes as he stared down the hill at the bridge. A bunch of farmers and storekeepers in homespun—how dull and shabby they looked against the splendid British soldiers in scarlet coats! His heart was in his throat as he watched them. Didn't they realize they'd be captured and hanged for this, every single one of them? Was freedom worth *that* much to them? He realized that tears were running down his cheeks and that he had bitten his lip until it was bleeding. He had no idea why he was crying except that he knew the red-haired captain was among them. And then a strange thing happened.

The firing suddenly stopped, and in this abrupt and unexpected silence Jed heard the bells again, this time coming from several directions at once. Surely those bells to the east came from Lexington? He had already heard the bells of Bedford. The others must be ringing at Watertown and Acton and Woburn. The sound of them echoed through the hills, carried to him by the same April wind that ruffled the grass at his feet. Now he knew why they were ringing. Jed thought of the red-haired captain and of all the men he had seen drilling in the villages around Boston. These bells were ringing for them. They were saying, "We're in trouble; we need you; snatch up a musket and come quickly, for this is the day it begins." And the message of the bells would bring more men to fight—and more and more and more. The British might have uniforms and a general and a King but they did not have the bells of Massachusetts on their side.

Jed wiped the tears from his cheeks and leaned forward to watch the bridge again, his face eager. He had promised Mr. Box he would take no sides in this quarrel but he knew he could never keep that promise now. If he'd had a musket he would have run down this hill to fight the redcoats, too. He realized he must hurry back and tell Mr. Box how wrong he was. He must make him understand about the bells.

When the firing stopped and the smoke cleared from the bridge below, the militia had stood their ground. It was the British redcoats who retreated. They were limping back into Concord with their wounded.

9

❧ Jed hurried away from Concord, impatient to reach Boston and share his news with Mr. Box. He went by way of the fields so that he would meet no soldiers on his way. Near Cambridge he was overtaken by a man on horseback who took him up on his horse to ride with him. It was late afternoon when they crossed the Neck and reached the town gates. While the man stopped to talk to the guards Jed slipped past and ran for Water Street.

But he was not to tell Mr. Box about the fighting today, after all. The shop was empty and dark. Jed called out, "Mr. Box! Mr. Box, where are you?"

From the kitchen Hovey said in a dull voice, "He's gone."

"Hovey, are you there?" called Jed excitedly. He ran into the kitchen to find that room dark, too. "Hovey, I have the most surprising news. There's been fighting in Concord—I saw it." While he spoke he reached for the lantern and with flint and tinder tried to strike a light. "Hovey, I wish you could have seen it. The militia fired on the redcoats—the *militia* did, Hovey!—and they drove the redcoats back. All over the countryside the church bells were ringing —rallying the militia from everywhere—and how the redcoats will ever get back to Boston town now I don't know!" The wick caught, and a feeble light flickered and then grew. He turned to see Hovey slumped at the trestle table. "Why, Hovey," he faltered, "what's the matter? I've never seen you look so. Are you sick?"

Hovey lifted a haggard face. "Sick?" he said, blinking at the light. "Sick? I ought to be--I deserve to be."

Jed looked around him. The hearth-fire was cold. He felt the embers. There had been no fire for a day or more. "Hovey," he said, "where's Mr. Box?"

"In jail."

"Jail!" gasped Jed. "Oh Hovey, no—how can that be?"

Hovey shook his great head and a sob escaped him. "Aye, he's in jail and 'tis my fault, I own it. My

fault! If only I'd listened to him!" He put his head back into his arms.

"What do you mean?" cried Jed. "How did they find out about him?"

Hovey wearily lifted his head. "I passed some o' the bills. He always said never in Boston, but I ran out o' money one night last week, and stopped for some ale—and nothing happened, so I passed some more the next night."

Jed sat down opposite him at the table. "Oh, Hovey," he said.

Hovey nodded. "They come for him the night you left for Bedford—no more'n an hour or two afterward, it must have been. I saw them leave the shop with him—and there he is in jail and has been for two nights and a day."

Jed's heart sank. "Oh, Hovey," he whispered reproachfully.

"And they took both his presses away, and all those beautiful copper-plates he made for printing money, and they say them wot get arrested these days gets no trial in Boston town. It's the new law —they're sent to England for trial."

"England!" exclaimed Jed. "Oh, Hovey, he mustn't be sent to England. Why, we'd never see him again."

Hovey said tiredly, "Well, there's naught we can do about it now."

"There must be," cried Jed, the thought of the fighting in Concord wiped from his mind. "We've money now—I brought back real money from Mr. Andrews in Bedford, you know. There must be something we can do for him with that money."

Hovey's eyes brightened. "Money, eh? I'd forgotten about that. How much? Bring it out and let's count it."

Jed hesitated. Hovey's eyes were shining and there was a sudden eagerness about him that Jed didn't like. For the first time he looked at Hovey as if he was a stranger, remembering that once Hovey had come near to strangling him. It was Hovey, after all, who had foolishly and needlessly given Mr. Box away. Jed had the oilskin packet of money in his pocket but he decided it was dangerous to tell Hovey so. "I don't know," he lied, crossing his fingers. "I was afraid of being searched at the gates, so I buried it under a tree on the Roxbury road."

Hovey seemed to believe him—at least the eagerness died from his eyes. "You shouldn't have," he told Jed with a shake of his head. "You'll forget where you buried it."

Jed stood up. "I'll go and get it now, Hovey. It's nearly dark—see?—and I'll be able to slip in and out without anyone seeing me."

"Aye, do that—there's a good lad." The eagerness came back to Hovey's eyes. He jumped up and laid his arm across Jed's shoulders. "And bring it straight back here to me, boy, for I'm in command now." He walked with Jed toward the door, his arm heavy on his shoulders.

Jed was sure by now that Hovey did not plan to spend any money on Mr. Box. No, nor on Jed, either. It was the money Hovey wanted and then he would be off to another colony with it. "Yes," agreed Jed—anything to get away from Hovey's hands and put the money in a safe place. "What prison have they taken him to, Hovey?"

"The one in town, on Prison Lane."

Jed brightened. At least they had not taken him to the prison ship in Boston harbor—not yet, anyway. There might still be a way to see him and talk to him, and Mr. Box would know what to do.

Hovey opened the door for him. "I'll be waiting here, Jed," he said in a voice like honey, and patted him on the cheek. "Mind you hurry back, now."

Jed nodded and walked into the street. He looked back only once, at the corner, to make sure that Hovey wasn't following him. But it was dark and after curfew, and dangerous to be on the streets. He saw Hovey close the door and blow out the lantern.

Now he had to think of a place to hide the package of money he carried, and find a place to sleep for the night. After a few minutes of wandering he remembered the little garden behind the print shop. For as long as Jed had lived with Mr. Box nobody had ever walked beyond the hogshead that stored rain water; yet it was a long garden, running all the way back to the lane behind it. Jed stole quietly around corners until he reached that lane.

The fence was half rotted and he squeezed through it into Mr. Box's garden. With his hands he dug a hole at the bottom of a cherry tree. When he had buried the money in its oilskin packet he scattered twigs across the spot. Taking care not to make any sound or to show himself, he went off to sleep on the ground in the Common.

The next morning everyone in Boston learned of the fighting that Jed had seen, and Jed learned more.

The first shots had been fired in Lexington, which the British troops passed through at dawn on their way to Concord. Eight American men had been killed there on the village green before the British exchanged shots with the militia at the North Bridge in Concord. But what brought triumph to Jed's heart was that the fight had not ended at the bridge where he had heard the bells. Those redcoats had begun to march back to Boston a few hours later, and the militia had fought them all the way back along the roads. They had lain behind stone walls and hidden in barns and farmhouses, and they had kept firing at the British soldiers until the troops broke and ran.

Those British troops were now across the bay in Charlestown. People said General Gage was afraid to bring them back into Boston lest people see how many redcoats he had lost.

War had begun.

10

❧ Overnight Boston changed. The British troops
marched back, but this time to stay, because General
Gage had lost too many officers to attack the rebels
right away. What he did was begin arresting all the
rebel leaders who remained in Boston town. They
were packed off at once to prison ships in the harbor.
He couldn't arrest the children or wives of these men,
so he gave them passes to leave town. In exchange
the Americans gave passes through their lines to any
Tories outside of Boston who wanted to live near
the British. Soon the streets were full of carts loaded
with bedding and pots and pans, half of them rebel

families leaving Boston and half of them Tory families coming into Boston. Both sides wondered when they would see their homes again.

Jed went back to the shop only once, but he didn't linger even when he found Hovey gone. For a week he wandered the streets, too young to be noticed or questioned. A woman leaving Boston gave him a loaf of bread and a rind of cheese. "They're allowing no food to leave Boston," she told him sadly. "Better you have it than the redcoats." Hundreds of houses were left empty. One night Jed crawled through a broken window into a kitchen and found a smoked ham and a handful of raisins. He lived on the ham for days.

At the end of the second week he saw Mr. Box.

He would not have seen Mr. Box at all if he hadn't thought of using half of Mr. Box's money to bribe a guard. He dug up the oilskin packet and went off to Prison Lane with it. The British guard on duty was hungry—everyone was hungry in Boston—and Mr. Box was not listed as a rebel or a spy but as a common criminal. The soldier knew where he could buy a turkey if he had enough money. He took Jed's bills and led him down a dark, damp staircase. At the bottom, behind an iron grating, sat Mr. Box and a dozen other men. There was very little light and no fresh air. The smells very nearly made Jed sick.

"Jed!" gasped Mr. Box, stumbling to his feet, and his astonishment warmed Jed's heart.

"Five minutes—not a second longer," the guard said sternly.

Mr. Box limped to the grating and stared at Jed. "I can't believe my eyes."

Jed couldn't, either. This was a different Mr. Box, dirty and unshaved. His eyes were red from lack of sleep, his shirt was soiled and his coat torn. "Oh, Mr. Box," Jed said in pity. But pity would do Mr. Box no good at all and they had only five minutes. He brightened and smiled. "So much has happened, Mr. Box—oh, but I've missed you," he told him. "First, here's the money that Mr. Andrews gave me in Bedford. I used half of it to bribe the guard —I hope you don't mind—but I thought it would make your time easier here to have the money that's left."

"Bless you," said Mr. Box, and took the money eagerly through the bars. "It's terrible here, terrible —so many prisoners coming in every day, and nothing to eat." He straightened suddenly, as if remembering that Jed had never seen him like this before. In his old manner he said, "You're a good boy, Jed. I won't be here long, you know."

"No, of course not," said Jed politely.

"A man of my talents—" Mr. Box rubbed his eyes with a dirty hand. "Dreadful place, Jed. They dare not keep me long. What on earth's happening in Boston town that they have no time to hear my story?"

"So many things," Jed cried eagerly. "There's been fighting—it began in Lexington two weeks ago. There are only Tories left in Boston now—Tories and redcoats. The King still won't change anything,

and so they say there will have to be a real war now between the British and the Americans."

Mr. Box sighed. "A fine time for them to begin their fighting, with me in prison. Why couldn't they have started their ridiculous revolt another time? Stubborn and selfish, that's what these rebels are."

"Oh no, Mr. Box—please," Jed said excitedly. "I saw it begin; I really did. The bells rang all over the countryside—it was the grandest thing! They just may lick the British, Mr. Box—really they may."

"Hush," said Mr. Box sharply. "Good heavens, you say that *here?* You'll be in jail, too, if they hear you. As for licking the British—impossible. These upstarts have no money, no uniforms, no generals, nothing."

"But they have courage," pointed out Jed. "It takes that to fight a king, doesn't it, Mr. Box?"

Mr. Box said sternly, "Jed, I'm not a political man. I refuse to listen to you or argue with you. All I ask is to get back to my shop and be a printer again. Yes, a printer," he said firmly. "They may call me a counterfeiter, but I'm a printer by trade."

"Yes, sir," said Jed.

"And the British will win. They have the King of England behind them—and England is the greatest empire since Rome. You're a boy and don't know about things like this. The underdog appeals to you, but mark my words, m'boy—underdogs never win. Kings and armies win. Money wins."

Jed said hotly, "Then you've never been

whipped or starved by a cruel master, to say that."

Mr. Box looked at him in mild surprise. He smiled a little. "You'd be surprised at what I've endured, Jed. That's how I've learned to smell out the winning side."

Jed stubbornly shook his head. "If you could have been with me—if you could have heard the bells ringing——"

But Mr. Box wasn't listening. "By hook or by crook I'll get out," he said, his eyes bright. "Yes, by hook or by crook I'll be out of this jail before the month is over, Jed. If you see Hovey tell him so."

Jed sighed. "Yes, Mr. Box." He didn't tell him that Hovey had deserted him. Mr. Box had enough to worry about.

"That's a promise, Jed—before the month is out."

The guard was coming down the stairs. Mr. Box said quickly, "Keep yourself alive somehow, m'boy. I'll find you—don't worry about that. And bless you for coming—you're a better friend to me than Hovey."

"Thank you, sir," said Jed.

He left the prison sadly. Mr. Box was the best friend he had, Mr. Box was his master and Jed was bound out to him for five years. He did wish he could make Mr. Box understand how he felt. He did wish Mr. Box would listen to him.

Was Mr. Box right about the smallness of the rebels' chance? Grown-ups had a tiresome way of

being right. Had British soldiers never been defeated?
He thought about it carefully all day. He walked
down to the harbor where he could watch the redcoats at work on Fort Hill. They had plenty of
cannons, all right. He followed Kirby Street back to
Fish and then Ship Street, and watched the redcoats
busy at the North Battery. After a while he walked
out toward the town gate and watched the redcoats
working on the fortifications there. Everywhere Boston was being turned into a fort.

He told himself that the province of Massachusetts was large, with a great many men ready to fight
—but he knew none of those men were trained to
fight as an army, like the British.

He reminded himself that the British soldiers
were thousands of miles away from home—yet England was rich, and could send dozens of ships to Boston full of guns and food and more soldiers.

To comfort himself, Jed walked down to Ferry
Way and stared out across the Charles River. He
wondered if the Americans were still camped around
Boston town. He wondered what would happen next.

11

❧ Mr. Box had told Jed to keep alive in Boston somehow, but this wasn't easy to do. There was little
enough food in town for people who could pay for
it, and Jed had no money at all. For two weeks he
made his home in an empty barn on Summer Street.
He took food where he could find it—cherries from
a tree on Milk Street, potatoes from the cellar of an
abandoned house, scraps of meat begged from a tavern's kitchen. Then one day it occurred to him that
Boston was surrounded by water—if he could make
a fishing rod and find a hook he might try his luck
at fishing from a wharf. The very thought of catch-
ing something made his mouth water. Then he re-

membered the rowboat that Hovey had used to get
him in and out of Boston town. Hovey was gone.
He had probably taken the boat with him, but it
wouldn't hurt to find out.

Jed set out at night, long after curfew so no one
would see him. He was fairly nimble now at dodging
sentries and the night watch. He stole through the
dark streets and the Common to the small, forgotten
dock that Hovey had shown him. In the faint moonlight the water looked like black ink. Jed lay down
and felt under the dock. He found the rope and
pulled it. To his astonishment the rowboat was still
attached to the end of it. The boat floated out and
then drifted back under the dock.

Jed stood up, excited at his luck. This was a
treasure he'd never hoped for. A boat meant that he
could go fishing any time he pleased. It meant that
he could leave Boston any time he wanted. Then he
realized that the boat was too valuable for fishing,
because if the redcoats saw it they might take it away
from him. He would keep it here, hidden.

He walked back toward town, a little careless
now about keeping among the shadows. He had forgotten his hunger. His mind was on the boat and its
possibilities. As he came to Marlborough Street he
stopped to look to the right and to the left, and
bumped squarely into another shadow that had paused
there, too. Jed let out a yelp of surprise.

"Ssh," hissed the shadow. "You want the soldiers to hear you?"

The moon suddenly came out from behind a cloud and shone for a second on a face that was familiar. Jed gasped, "I've seen you before!" The moon had disappeared but he knew that bright yellow hair and freckled face. Where had he seen it before?

"Yes, and I know you," said the boy. "You're the lad who would take no sides. You've taken sides now," he added grimly, "or you'd not be in Boston town still."

"That's not true," Jed said hotly. "I'm here because my master's in jail. I remember your name now —Ben Wheeler."

"I wish you didn't have such a good memory," said the boy. "I wish I could believe you, too, about not being a Tory."

"Well, I'm not," snapped Jed. "I delivered a message to Paul Revere once—and I saw the fighting begin at Concord."

The boy laughed. "What kind of talk is that? Anyone could deliver a message to Paul Revere when he was in Boston."

"Yes, but I took it to him from Cambridge. It came from a man I met there in the middle of the night."

"Who was he?" demanded Ben.

"I don't know his name, but he had red hair and a friend named Tim. And he said if ever he had need of me again his message would come from the 'red-haired captain.'"

"Hmmm," said Ben thoughtfully.

"You know him?" asked Jed eagerly. "Do you come from over there?" He pointed toward the bay.

Ben said, "I'd be a fool to trust you, wouldn't I?"

Jed sighed. "I suppose so." He looked at Ben shrewdly. "But you were sneaking through the streets just as I was—and we can both be arrested for being out after curfew."

"True enough," admitted Ben. "All right, I'll confess I came from over there. My father's in the militia."

"Then do tell me what's happening," begged Jed.

The boy looked around them carefully and drew Jed deeper into the shadows. "Where can I find you?" he asked. "If I should want to talk to you again. Or if," he added slowly, "your 'red-haired captain' has need of you."

"Then you do know him!"

"Maybe."

Jed told him about the barn on Summer Street, and Ben nodded. "But can't you tell me something of what's going on outside Boston?" he begged.

"I'll tell you this much," said Ben. "We've captured Fort Ticonderoga. Not a bad start for a war, is it?"

Jed had no idea what or where Fort Ticonderoga was, but he agreed that capturing it was a splendid thing.

"I'll say goodbye now," whispered Ben. "If you

speak of meeting me to anyone, I'll learn of it—you understand? So don't."

"But of course I won't," Jed said. "Don't you believe me?"

"Maybe I do and maybe I don't—it's not for me to decide," said Ben. "Goodbye for now, Jed, and don't follow me."

Jed watched him zigzag through the shadows and disappear. He shivered with excitement. Ben must be in Boston town on some errand the British mustn't know about. Perhaps it even had something to do with the rebel militia camped outside of town. It made him feel less lonely, somehow, for with Mr. Box in prison and his stomach always empty it was becoming harder and harder for Jed to remember the bells at Concord. . . .

A few days later Jed was lucky enough to find a job. He stopped at a tavern on Ship Street to beg for food and the woman gave him a slice of duck pie and looked him over sternly. "Hungry?"

"Yes, ma'am."

"Who do you belong to?"

"To Mr. Titherming Box of Water Street—but he's in prison just now, ma'am."

"Hmph." Her eyes narrowed. "Well, it happens I've need of a boy to sweep the tavern and empty out slops. If you work for me I'll give you three meals a day."

"I can begin right now," Jed said eagerly.

"Not big meals," she added sternly. "There's little enough food to go 'round. But I guess I can spare some from what I put on *their* plates."

Jed soon learned that when she said *their* or *them* she meant the redcoats.

"*They're* here tonight," she would say with a sniff. Or, "I've a nice chicken today, Jed. Eat as much as you please before I send it in to *them*." After she and Jed had eaten the chicken, strange things would happen to it. Suddenly it would have too much salt in it, or red pepper instead of black; but only the bravest of soldiers dared to complain. It took courage to face Mrs. Muffet's cold, stern eye. She was a rebel at heart and would gladly have left Boston with the other rebels, but she was a widow and the *Ship's Mermaid* was all that she owned in the world. She stayed behind to protect it.

Jed still slept in the empty barn, waking up each day to walk through the streets to the *Ship's Mermaid*. The harbor was full of British ships guarding Boston, and the rebels held the land all around Boston. General Gage had said he would pardon every man who had fought at Lexington and Concord— every man except John Hancock and Sam Adams, anyway—if they would just throw down their muskets and go home. But nobody did this. The British did nothing, either.

Then one dawn people began running past the *Ship's Mermaid* toward Lynn Street and Hudson's Point. Jed could hear their feet on the cobbles. He

had just arrived at the tavern and was sweeping the
floor. Mrs. Muffet went outside in her apron and demanded to know what was going on. A moment later
she put her head in the door and called to Jed, "Hurry
—something's happening. Forget the sweeping!"

They left the tavern and ran with the others—
women, small children, and one man still in his night-
cap. When they reached the water they stopped and
looked across the river. From Charlestown the land

ran out into the harbor in a long, low line, to end in
two hills where cows usually grazed on pleasant summer days. There were no cows this morning. At the
top of the lower hill—called Breed's Hill—the rebels
had been digging earthworks during the night. The
rail fences that had kept cattle from wandering onto
Bunker's Hill had been stuffed with hay so that men
could be concealed behind them. Jed could see people working there—digging, piling more rocks on

the low stone walls and carrying hay. It was the first he had seen of the rebel militia since he had left Concord. It gave him a thrill to realize they were still nearby, and had been so all the time.

"Well, now," said Mrs. Muffet with satisfaction. "This is more like it."

"What does it mean?" he asked.

Mrs. Muffet gave a slow smile. "It's like they're thumbing their noses at General Gage, Jed. He can't let them build earthworks right under his eyes. He'll have to stop them."

"There'll be fighting, then?"

"Aye, I should think so." She sighed. "Say a prayer for the men over there, Jed. They've little to fight with but spirit and gumption."

As they stood watching, a puff of smoke burst from the cannon of a British warship in the harbor. A minute later they heard the sound of it and saw another puff against the bright blue sky. The cannons from the fort on Copp's Hill began firing on Breed's Hill, too, and Jed covered his ears.

"There'll be no business done today," said Mrs. Muffet with a sigh. She turned and scanned the tall houses behind them. "The Widow Moore lives there," she said, pointing. "We'll watch from one of her upstairs windows. It's been a long time since I've paid her a call."

But it was noon before the British soldiers were ready to march down to the wharves to be loaded on barges. Seeing them, Jed felt sorry for them—they

carried so much on their backs. It was one of the hot-
test summer days Boston town had seen so far, and
every redcoat was bent nearly double under a heavy
pack. One by one the barges began to move. There
were no bells ringing today—only the tiresome roar
of British cannons and the feeble roll of drums. On
the other side of the river, on Breed's Hill, Jed could
see men walk down the slope carrying muskets. They
would vanish behind a rail fence or a pile of stones.
There didn't seem to be a great number of them.
They didn't march down the hill as an army would.
No great cannons were firing from the rebel earthworks—the rebels didn't have any.

"Bunch of farmers," shouted a Tory from the
street below, and everybody laughed.

The first barge landed at the bottom of Breed's
Hill. Its redcoats got out and marched away out of
sight. The second wave of redcoats landed and
formed a parade line near the water, their coats bright
against the soft green of the meadows.

"Oh dear—Charlestown's on fire," said Mrs.
Muffet, pointing to flames and smoke pouring from
behind the hill. But aside from cannons setting fire
to Charlestown nothing happened for a while. Then
suddenly the smoke of muskets rose from the other
side of the hill.

"They're attacking over there," said Mrs. Muffet grimly.

"Yes, and look—they're going to attack on this
side of the hill, too!" cried Jed.

The redcoats still on the beach had formed into smart lines and now they began to climb the gentle slope of the hill. They climbed slowly. In the heat they did not look real, for they were so far away they looked like clusters of red ants on the move. When they neared the earthworks at the top, a hundred rebel muskets seemed to go off at once. The red line faltered and a number of men did not move again. The ones still walking hurried back down the hill.

Mrs. Muffet said, "It's General Howe's men who are fighting on the other side, where we can't see them. These must be General Pigot's men."

If that was so, thought Jed, then General Howe's regiment was attacking again and again, for the smoke from their muskets was turning the sky gray. Down on the shore Pigot's men were working over cannons that had bogged down in the mud. Jed heard a woman in the street say, "I don't see why it's taking so long. I thought those rebels would run away at first sight of the British."

Her husband said sourly, "Well, they didn't."

It was late in the afternoon when General Howe's men marched into view again from the other side of the hill. To Jed this was good news. It meant that General Howe's attacks on the other side of the hill had failed. The Americans must have driven the British back at every new attempt.

The two forces rallied now and together went up the hill toward the earthworks. The rebels fired

when the lines neared the top, and redcoat after redcoat toppled over in the hot afternoon sunshine. But
this time the British fell back for only a minute. They
attacked again, and suddenly there was no more firing
from the earthworks and the British disappeared over
the top.

"Lord love us," said Mrs. Muffet with a shudder.

"What happened? What went wrong?" cried
Jed, not wanting to believe that the redcoats had
taken the hill.

"Sounds to me like the Americans ran out of
gunshot," said Mrs. Muffet, and there were tears in
her eyes. Angrily she blew her nose and sniffed.

A great cheer went up from the crowds in the
street below. The British had captured the hill. Never
mind if it had taken all afternoon, or if the rebels
could still get away across Charlestown Neck—the
British had won the battle.

It was night when the barges returned to Boston
town, and there were no drums rolling now. By the
flickering light of lanterns Jed and Mrs. Muffet stood
and watched the British unload their wounded. There
were hundreds—perhaps more than a thousand—so
many that the wounded had to be left on the wharves
for the night because there was nowhere else to place
them. It was Jed's first glimpse of sick and dying
men and he shuddered in horror.

After an hour of watching Mrs. Muffet drew

him away. "It's no sight for a boy to see," she told him quietly. "Enough is enough."

But when they at last reached the tavern she said, with her usual sniff, "So the hill belongs to *them* now, and I certainly hope they're happy about it, for it looks to me as if they lost half their army taking it." She added spitefully, "A few more victories like that and they'll lose the war!"

12

❧ The church bells of Boston town had always tolled for funerals. After the fighting at Breed's Hill there were so many funerals the bells tolled all day long until General Gage ordered them to be silent. Still the wounded kept dying, and Boston was a dismal, mournful town. This battle of Breed's Hill was not a victory the British could celebrate.

One night, sound asleep in his barn, Jed was awakened by a tap on his shoulder. He sat up in alarm. He would have cried out, but a hand flew to his mouth and covered it.

"Ssh, it's me," said Ben Wheeler in a low voice.

"I'm certainly glad to see you, but you scared me half to death," gasped Jed.

"I've a message for you from the Red-Haired Captain, Jed—except he's a major now."

"Really?" Jed put both hands to his eyes to rub the sleep away. "So he's a major now? That means he must have fought on Breed's Hill and fought well. He wasn't wounded?" he asked quickly.

"No, we didn't lose half the men the British did."

"But you lost the hill. The rebels haven't given up, have they?"

Ben's grin was white in the moonlight that came through the barn window. "Not on your life," he said. "Did you think we would? Oh, that was a bad fight for everyone, and the rebels were discouraged about it at first. But what did they really lose except one hill they had no need of, anyway? 'Tis the British who lost more. Did you think we couldn't hear the bells tolling when the wind was right?"

"You're not funning me?" said Jed hopefully.

Ben shook his head. "No sir. The British may have won that hill all right, but we showed 'em we could fight a real battle. I don't think they expected that. We showed 'em we're soldiers and now they know what they're up against. And I'll tell you another thing, Jed—the other colonies are sending men now. It gave them heart, too—to know we could fight like that against the British army."

"What other colonies?"

"Why, men from Pennsylvania and New York

and New Hampshire and Connecticut. More men are coming every day, Jed. And the Congress in Philadelphia has appointed a general, too. His name is George Washington. He's over there across the river figuring out what to do next."

This last bit of news particularly excited Jed. He remembered hearing Mr. Box say the rebels had no army and no general, no king and no money. Well, maybe they didn't have much money—and a king they didn't need—but they had an army and a general. His eyes sparkled. "Tell me the message from the Red-Haired Cap—I mean Major."

Ben moved closer in the straw and dropped his voice to a whisper. "The rebels have need of news from inside Boston, Jed. You know most of the rebels got away right after Lexington. Any rebel sympathizers that are still here can't get out. They're known and closely watched. The Red-Haired Major says, will you keep your eyes and ears open and help us?"

"Me?" gasped Jed.

Ben nodded. "Why not?" He hesitated. "Your master's still in jail?"

"Yes," said Jed, "but I was able to see him. He says he'll be out soon."

Ben looked at him pityingly. "Jed, they're not letting people out of jail. He said that only to cheer you up. The prisons are terrible places these days. I don't want to be cruel, but if I were you I wouldn't expect to see him again. Certainly not for years."

In his heart Jed knew he was right, but he

wouldn't admit it. He said doggedly, "What about the Major's message?"

"He wants your help. The rebels have to know what the British are doing."

"But they won't tell *me*," pointed out Jed.

"No, but you can listen and you can watch. Who would suspect you? You're a boy whose master is in jail and you're hanging around waiting and hoping to see him. Nobody will notice you. You can watch for little things. For instance, the ovens going all night at army headquarters could mean bread being baked for a march out of town in the morning. If a ship comes into the harbor you can tell us whether it brings new soldiers, and how many, and what regiments."

Jed thought about it and nodded. "Yes, I could do that," he said soberly. "I didn't tell you yet that I sweep and clean now for the Widow Muffet on Ship Street. A good many redcoats come there. I can listen to what they say."

Ben's eyes widened. "Wonderful! Oh, you'll do a capital job, Jed."

"But if the redcoats plan to march—to fight, or anything important—how would I reach you and the Major in time?"

"We'll get you a boat."

"I have a boat."

Ben stared at him in astonishment. "You have? Already you've the wits of a spy, Jed. Good for you."

So he would be a spy. That sounded fun.

"The Red-Haired Major says, do you remember the house across the river where you met?"

Jed nodded.

"There's always someone there at night now. If you have terribly important news you can row there by dark. Otherwise I'm to stop here once a week to see you. And if you're not here at the barn I'll look for you at the Widow Muffet's." He looked at Jed and frowned. "It's awfully important, Jed."

"Of course—I know that."

Ben said slowly, "But you don't know *how* important. If General Gage should decide to fight tomorrow I think the Americans would have to give up, Jed."

"It's that bad?"

Ben nodded. "We ran out of ammunition at Breed's Hill; there just wasn't anything left to shoot. We need time. . . . Above all, we need to know their plans."

Jed swore a silent oath to find out what he could.

Ben turned to go and then stopped. "I nearly forgot—here's a remembrance for you." He slid into Jed's hand what felt like a square of cardboard.

Jed held it up to the moonlight. "What is it?" he asked.

"Continental money. Mr. Paul Revere has set up his press at Watertown. This is the new money. Not British money—*American* money."

Jed's expert eye studied it and he smiled a little. "Not awfully well done," he said politely.

"I know," Ben said gloomily. "The paper's terrible—it doesn't take ink very well."

Jed thought of what Mr. Box would say of it if he could see it. "A botched job," he'd say. "Throw it into the fire, m'boy!"

"It'll get better when we can make finer paper," Ben assured him. "You can't buy anything with it in Boston town, of course, but I brought it along to show you. You may keep it if you'd like," he added generously.

"Thank you very much," said Jed. It was his first present and he slid it into the pocket of his trousers.

"I'll see you here a week from tonight," Ben said, and walked out of the barn.

The next morning Jed changed his route to the Widow Muffet's tavern. He decided he might help the red-haired major by seeing as much of Boston as possible every day. By getting up an hour earlier, and by checking different streets on his way to the tavern he might be able to get a picture of what the British were doing. Once a day he would take a look at the Common, where a good many redcoats camped, and once a day he would pass Province House, where General Gage made his headquarters. From the Widow Muffet's he could keep an eye on the harbor and the islands around Boston, and at the tavern he could also listen to what the British officers and men were saying. This seemed the most that he could manage for now, but he expected to think of new ways later.

He was determined to be the very best of spies.

13

❧ It was a hot July and an even hotter August, but the gardens of Boston bloomed. The Widow Muffet had a large kitchen garden and each morning Jed picked green beans, peas, tomatoes, chard, corn and carrots for her. But there was no meat. Boston was a town and its meat had always come from the country around it. On market days before the fighting began, the road across the Neck had been filled with sheep and cows and pigs being driven into town, and with carts bringing in smoked meats, live chickens, eggs and venison. Now the road was closed and there was only the sea and its fish.

By midsummer the last milk-cows in Boston were being killed for their meat. This meant no more milk. General Gage sent ships out to make raids up and down the coast but the livestock they captured and brought back went to the army and neither Jed nor Mrs. Muffet saw any of it.

"What worries me," said the widow, "is the thought of winter." She was standing over a kettle making birch beer, boiling its roots and its bark together and adding to it the last of her maple syrup and some leftover apple parings. "You think you're tired of fish now—it'll be all there is to eat when winter comes. And how will people keep warm?"

"Why, with—" Jed stopped and frowned. He'd forgotten that wood and coal also came over the road to Boston town. He glanced out of the kitchen window to the birches standing in the widow's back yard.

"Aye," said Mrs. Muffet, following his gaze. "Pretty, aren't they? But I doubt they'll be there by next spring. Gone for kindling, more likely, and that'll be the end of my birch beer.

"Bad days," she added with a sigh, "and to make it worse I hear there's sickness everywhere."

"What kind of sickness?"

"Who knows? It's from the heat—and everybody crowded in here together, and not enough to eat. It's not a natural way to live. The only comfort to me is that the soldiers are feeling it just like you and me."

Jed pricked up his ears. Here was news to give Ben Wheeler. "The soldiers are sick, too?"

"Land sakes, of course they are—they're human beings, aren't they? And just as hungry as everybody else. I hear half of the Royal Light Dragoons have come down with the flux—half of 'em!"

Yes, this was news for Ben Wheeler. He nearly jumped as someone rang the bell in the tavern room. The widow said, "You go, Jed. I've got the birch beer to tend, and huckleberry pies in the oven."

Jed put down the potatoes he was paring and walked into the tavern room. Its walls were darkened with age and chimney smoke and the windows opening on the street were small. So little daylight came in that at first he didn't see the man who was standing at the bar. Then he heard a chuckle from the shadows and as Jed spun around the man walked forward.

"Well now, m'boy," said Mr. Box, smiling at him and showing his square white teeth. "I told you I'd get out of jail, didn't I? And here I am, and I've had the devil's own time finding you, I can tell you that."

"*Mr. Box!*" gasped Jed. It was like seeing a ghost. He couldn't believe his eyes.

"Surprised you, haven't I?" Mr. Box was beaming.

"Surprised me!" echoed Jed, and with a laugh flew into his arms. "I thought I'd never see you again. I thought they'd put you on a prison ship, or send you to England, or hang you!" He drew back to look at his master. "You're clean again!" he said, smiling.

"Aye—clean again and a new man. I've lost my plumpness but gained my freedom—even if it did take longer than I promised you." He patted Jed fondly. "Now let me look at you." He held him at arms' length and inspected him. "I think you've eaten better than I from the looks of you, m'boy."

From the kitchen doorway the Widow Muffet said gruffly, "And why not, with Mary Muffet to feed him? I've had no complaints yet about my cooking, thank you."

Jed cried joyfully, "Mrs. Muffet, this is Mr. Box! They've let him out of jail."

"Land sakes; then he must be hungry," said the widow. "Fetch him something to drink, Jed, while I cut a pie for him. Come into the kitchen, Mr. Box, and I'll dish out some stew for you."

"That's very kind of you," said Mr. Box.

She sniffed. "It's worth a celebration when *they* let someone out of jail." She stole a quick look at him. "And what did they put a fine gentleman like you in jail for?"

Jed looked at Mr. Box and Mr. Box looked at Jed. "I—uh—printed the wrong things in my shop," he said weakly.

The Widow Muffet nodded, and Jed knew she thought Mr. Box had been printing pamphlets for the rebels. He couldn't help wishing that it had been for this reason Mr. Box was arrested.

"There now, I shouldn't be asking you questions when you're as empty as a sack. Sit right down," said Mrs. Muffet, placing a bowl of hot stew on the table.

"When you've finished call me and I'll cut a pie for you. Sit with him, Jed. I'll sweep the tavern for you." She bustled out of the kitchen, leaving the two of them alone.

Jed smiled shyly at Mr. Box. "She's been very good to me, sir. How does it happen they let you out, Mr. Box? It's just a miracle."

He thought Mr. Box looked a little uncomfortable, but perhaps he was wrong. "Why, they found the time to listen to me," he said easily. "It seems they need printers, so many of them having left Boston town, and so—here I am."

"But that's wonderful," said Jed.

"Not only that," continued Mr. Box, "but they're giving me back my press and my shop."

Jed's mouth dropped open. "Your shop—and your press, too!" He stared at him in astonishment.

"Is that so strange? The important thing," said Mr. Box, waving a spoon at Jed, "is always to land on your feet—like a cat, my boy. Ever see a cat land on its head or its tail?"

"No sir," said Jed.

Mr. Box nodded. "Always on its feet. No bruises, no hurts—it's worth remembering. You can learn a great deal from a cat." He finished the stew and sat back. "You've not seen Hovey?"

Jed shook his head. "Only the once, sir, the day he told me you'd been arrested." He hesitated and then added, "Did you know he spent some of the false bills in Boston?"

Mr. Box placed a finger to his lips. "Not so

loudly, m'boy. Yes, they told me." He shook his head. "I fear that we'll see no more of Hovey. A pity."

The Widow Muffet came back into the kitchen with the broom. "There's one thing," she said with a scowl.

"Yes, Mrs. Muffet."

"Does this mean I'll be seeing no more of Jed? You'll be taking him away with you?"

Mr. Box glanced at his empty stew dish and then at Jed and he smiled. "Well now, that scarcely seems fair, Mrs. Muffet. Perhaps we could share him. What do you say to that?"

Mrs. Muffet blushed and her scowl deepened. "It would certainly be kind of you, seeing as how I've grown fond of the boy and seeing what a good worker he is as well."

Mr. Box nodded. "How about it, Jed?"

"I'd like that ever so much," he said eagerly.

"Good. I'll have need of you to find food and cook it for me, but that will scarcely keep you busy all day. You can sleep at the print shop and come to Mrs. Muffet as soon as you've finished your chores."

How kind Mr. Box was. Jed realized he would have missed Mrs. Muffet very much. He had four friends now—Mr. Box, the red-haired major, Ben Wheeler and the Widow Muffet.

"I'm obliged to you," said Mrs. Muffet with a nod, and her face softened. "I'll cut the pie now, and seeing as this is by way of a celebration I'll even sit down and have a piece of it myself."

14

They found the printing shop the same except for one pane of glass broken in the window. The very next day a British officer and two men arrived with a wheelbarrow on which sat one of Mr. Box's printing presses.

"Take it upstairs," Mr. Box told the officer. To Jed he explained, "There's more room up there. You'll be sleeping down here and I may have to work late at night."

The British officer came down the stairs, and noticing the broken window said, "I'll see that the glass is replaced at once. Anything else?"

"Some copper for engraving?"

"You'll find it with your tools upstairs."

As he and his men went out Jed made a face.
"One week they have you in prison, and the next
week they can't do enough for you!"

Mr. Box glanced at him sharply and then turned
away, saying with a shrug, "It's rather pleasant after
four months in their jail, m'boy. Rather pleasant indeed."

After this it became just like the old days, before
the fighting began. Jed had no idea what printing Mr.
Box did upstairs. He was so busy Jed saw him only at
mealtime. But this was just as well, for it left Jed with
time to roam around Boston and look for news to
give Ben Wheeler. It also gave him plenty of time to
help Mrs. Muffet at the *Ship's Mermaid*. He arose at
dawn every morning and cooked or baked what he
could find. Sometimes it was only a loaf of rye-an'-
Injun bread, with tea brewed from dried raspberry
leaves. After breakfast he would set out to hunt for
more food. Mr. Box appeared to have money these
days, but money couldn't buy food that didn't exist.
By September Jed had worked out a regular route.
There was an empty house on Summer Street with
an orchard behind it. He began picking its apples
when they were still green. There was an empty
house on School Street with a kitchen garden near its
back door. Others knew of it, too, but if he got there
early enough he could dig up a few potatoes and
roots. Then he would go to market. If he was lucky
he would bring home some flour and fresh fish. If his

luck was ordinary he would bring home flour and dried fish. If it was a bad day he would bring home only flour.

To Jed this siege of Boston had its ironic side. The British had not so long ago punished the Americans by cutting Boston off from the rest of the world. Now the shoe was on the other foot and it was the British who were surrounded and cut off. They still had the sea, but very few ships came in, and it was rumored that the rebels were capturing British ships before they reached Boston. But it wasn't fun being hungry.

"I brought you some cheese," Ben told Jed when they met one night. He would come now to the print shop and tap on the window, knowing Jed slept beside it. Then they would meet in the garden behind the shop and whisper in the dark.

Jed seized the cheese and took a bite, savoring the richness of it on his tongue. "Mmm," he murmured, putting the rest in his pocket. "Do you eat like this all the time outside of Boston, Ben?"

Ben said seriously, "It's not so bad. The army gets food first, but people bring sheep and cows from all over Massachusetts."

"Sheep and cows," repeated Jed wistfully.

"How bad is it getting here?" asked Ben.

"Bad enough," said Jed. "So many people are sick from dysentery and the flux there are at least ten funerals every day. And there's very little food coming in from England."

Ben nodded. "Anything else?"

"Yes. They say General Gage is still mad as a hornet over the rebels' burning Boston Light."

Ben chuckled. "That was a good raid, wasn't it? We land at night and burn it down; they start building it again and it's burned a second time. But are they planning anything, Jed? Have you heard any rumors?"

Jed shook his head. "From what I hear, the British stay as worried as you. They fear an attack any time. They live in fear of their shadows—afraid that when winter comes and the river freezes over General Washington will cross into Boston; afraid that fire boats may set fire to the town. Of the two I think they fear fire the more."

"Do they now!" said Ben. "Anything else?"

"Yes—four soldiers came down with smallpox two days ago. This I heard from talk at the Widow Muffet's."

Ben whistled faintly. "Smallpox! Four of them sick with it today means six of them sick tomorrow, and a dozen or more by next week. Mind you don't catch it, Jed."

Jed shivered. "It's what carried my mother off, Ben. It's a terrible thing. Will I be seeing you next week?"

Ben hesitated. "I've a job of work for you tomorrow night, Jed. I'll be needing your help if you can give it."

Jed brightened. "Help? Oh, gladly, Ben." He

felt a surge of excitement. Now at last he would dis-
cover what Ben did on his trips by night into Boston
town. "What can I do?"

Ben waved him farther away from the house and
deeper into the shadows. "It's like this, Jed. I smuggle
things out of Boston. Sometimes I swim across; sometimes I come by boat. After Breed's Hill most of the
rebels got away, but in such a hurry they had to leave
behind swords and pistols and clothing and money
and important papers. So I come into Boston by night
and smuggle these things out to them. But one man
had to leave behind his family."

Jed waited.

"That's what I've got to smuggle out tomorrow," Ben said. "A woman and two babies."

"Babies!" exclaimed Jed.

Ben nodded. "It's not going to be easy. If you refuse I'll understand."

"But how?"

"By boat. I was hoping by *your* boat."

"But to get them to a boat you'll have to smuggle
them through the streets!"

Ben nodded. "I know. . . . Two babies, and the
town full of redcoats!"

"Isn't there any other way?" asked Jed.

Ben sighed. "Not for a woman and two children.
There've been some men smuggled out in broad daylight on fishing boats, but a woman and her children
aren't likely to have a pass to go fishing. There's no
possible way to disguise a baby, either; and worst of

all, this woman and her children are important to the
British as hostages." He hesitated. "I might as well
tell you they're kin to the Red-Haired Major."

That changed it: in a second Jed forgot the
dangers and said firmly, "If they're relatives of his
I'll help. Tell me what to do."

"Wear dark clothes. Expect me about eleven.
I'll tap on your window as usual." As if afraid that
Jed might change his mind, Ben gave his arm a
squeeze and disappeared almost at once into the darkness.

Jed stole softly back through the kitchen. As he
entered the front room, the door to the street opened
and a man stole with equal softness into the shop.
"Hey," cried Jed, startled.

"Jed?" It was Mr. Box's voice.

Jed gasped. "Aye, it's me. You scared me, sir! I
thought you were asleep upstairs."

"Just out for a breath of fresh air," said Mr. Box
smoothly. He brushed past Jed and went up to his
room.

Jed stood and looked after him, perplexed. A
man did not casually walk the streets of Boston town
at two o'clock in the morning. He could be thrown
into jail for being out after curfew. Mr. Box had been
fully dressed, too, and since there had been no jan-
gling of bells when the door opened, he must have
taken care to remove the bells before he went out.
Jed wondered how many other nights Mr. Box had
stolen past his bench while he was sound asleep. It

seemed that Mr. Box had secrets, too. Jed wondered what they were.

The next morning the ground was white with the year's first frost, and summer was suddenly gone. The sun was warm during the day, but the frost came back at night. After Mr. Box went to bed, Jed lay on his bench and pretended to be asleep, but his heart beat quickly as he waited for Ben. He jumped when Ben tapped lightly on the window soon after eleven. Shivering a little, Jed tiptoed through the kitchen, opened the heavy wooden door and joined his friend in the garden. Together, without a word, they slipped through the fence into the lane behind the shop. There Ben stopped.

"There are redcoats out tonight," he whispered in Jed's ear. "Listen."

Jed heard the *clip-clop* of horses' hooves on cobbles, but they were some distance away and did not come nearer. Soon the noise disappeared into the night. Ben touched his arm. "I've a rope here," he said. "I've tied it around my waist. Take hold of one end so you won't lose me in the darkness. Stay just behind and take care not to walk on my heels. We're off to Hannover Street."

Twice they stopped. There were indeed a great number of soldiers in the streets. "We couldn't have chosen a worse time," Ben whispered in his ear. "I heard two redcoats say it's rumored the rebels have sneaked into Boston by way of the mill dam. These British are as jumpy as fleas."

There was a moon, but it was wrapped in clouds and gave no light. From time to time they could see the bright glimmer of lanterns ahead of them. The streets were narrow, and the light of one lantern would crawl up the walls of the houses on either side and throw leaping shadows up and down the street. Then Jed and Ben would take to their heels and find another lane. It took them a long time to reach Hannover.

"There's the house," whispered Ben, and untied the rope that held them together. He led Jed among elms and lilac bushes and around to the rear. Ben knocked softly on a door and it opened at once. The two boys went in.

A candle burned in a corner of the kitchen. By its light Jed saw a young woman wrapped in shawls and cloak. When she turned in the light, he saw that the shawls were wrapped around a baby that she carried in her arms. Her face was worried.

"You're late," she said in an anxious voice. "I gave them laudanum to make them sleep, but I gave it to them three hours ago. Will they stay quiet for another hour, do you think? Should I give them more? What should I do?"

It surprised Jed that the woman should turn to Ben, who was only a year older than he was. Ben said, "You gave them exactly the same amount you were supposed to?"

She nodded.

"They mustn't wake up," said Ben, "and yet too much of the drug would harm them." He was thinking about it, his face sober, and Jed realized that in the last few months Ben had changed. He had not noticed it before. He thought of Ben coming into Boston every week, ducking soldiers and Tories and stealing into empty houses in the dark. It couldn't be easy. Perhaps it wasn't so surprising, after all, that this woman should ask Ben's advice. Ben nodded at last. "We'll leave now and take the chance," he said firmly. "Mrs. Duncan, this is Jed Crane. Jed, you carry the baby and I'll take the two-year-old. But we've got to hurry before the children wake up."

Mrs. Duncan held out the baby to Jed, her eyes looking into his face. She must have wondered at the strangeness of this moment: herself and the babies in the hands of two young boys who would try to smuggle them out of town. But whatever she saw in Jed's face must have pleased her, for she gave him a bright smile and picked up the bundle of clothes she had tied into a knot. "His name is Paul," she said, pointing to the baby in Jed's arms. "He is named after my husband's friend Paul Revere."

"And her husband," said Ben, "is your Red-Haired Major."

Jed's eyes widened. "Do the British know that?"

Mrs. Duncan shook her head. "Not yet. They know me by another name, but they've been looking for me and they're growing suspicious. They questioned me again three days ago. I'm ready now," she said, and blew out the candle.

They closed the door behind them and left the house. Now they must somehow make their way down Treamount Street to Common Street, and then steal through the common toward the secret, out-of-the-way place where Hovey's boat was hidden. The Common was dangerous. British soldiers still camped there, and there were trenches dug among the trees. There were also sentries to guard the stores and sentries to guard the river. But it was the side nearest to Cambridge, and only a mile across. With two children and a woman there was no faster way to leave Boston.

They tried to move quickly, but this was difficult. It had been a long time since Jed had had enough to eat and he was not as strong as he had once been: the sleeping child in his arms felt as heavy as a rock. Mrs. Duncan's sack was heavy and she walked nearly bent over, while Ben carried the two-year-old in his arms. It troubled Jed that none of them could run if they had to. At each street they had to stop and let Mrs. Duncan rest a minute. Then something in her bundle began to rattle and they had to stop again. She reached into the sack and drew out a heavy silver candlestick. "The Americans need silver so badly," she whispered. "Must I leave it behind?"

Ben nodded. "I'm afraid so."

Now they turned off Treamount Street to approach the Common from a side street. Walking softly in single file, they came to the corner of Common Street and paused. Since Jed was first in line, it was he who stuck his head out to look up and down the street. He saw no one and took a step forward.

"Halt—who goes there?" sang out a man's voice.

With all his heart Jed longed to run. He heard
Mrs. Duncan give a low cry behind him. He heard
Ben gasp. Turning, he thrust the baby at Ben and
walked out alone into the street to answer the voice.

A British soldier walked out of the shadows with
musket and bayonet pointed at him. "Who are you?"
he demanded.

"J—J—Jed Crane, sir," stammered Jed.

The soldier peered closely at him. "A boy, eh?
And what might you be doing out so late? Curfew
rang four hours ago."

Jed nodded miserably. "I know." He only hoped
that his body blocked the soldier's view of the dark
street behind him. He hoped that somehow Ben and
Mrs. Duncan could slip away without him. "I was
out for food, sir. There's a garden where sometimes
there are potatoes—that is, if a person gets there first.
I was trying to get there first."

"Hungry, eh?" The soldier's voice was softer.
"Well, who isn't? I wouldn't mind a potato myself,
roasted over a fire and yellow with melted butter."
He sighed. "Lor', if I wasn't alone here on duty I'd
go with you."

Jed thanked his lucky stars the sentry couldn't
go.

"But you can't do it," the sentry said. "Not for
all the potatoes in the world. It's against the law.
Where d'ye live, boy?"

"Water Street."

"Well, go home now. If you don't, somebody'll

take you for one of those rebels and shoot you. Go
along now, straight home, and get your potatoes tomorrow."

"Yes, sir," said Jed humbly. "Thank you, sir."

"And don't try it again."

"No, sir." He turned around and crept down the
street where he had left Ben and Mrs. Duncan. There
was no sign of them. He was about to give them up
when he heard a low hiss and Ben emerged from behind a tree. "Good work," he whispered. "We'll
have to try a different street now to get to the
Common."

Only then did Jed realize how close they had
come to being discovered and he began to tremble.
He yearned to obey the soldier and go directly home
to bed. The thought of risking another dark street
made his strained nerves jump. "Yes," he said weakly.
"All right. I'm ready."

He took the sleeping baby and they set out
again, this time going so far to the south that Jed
feared they would see the town gates before they
turned back toward the common. Worse, the baby
Jed carried began to stir and whimper in his sleep.

"They're both so hungry," whispered Mrs.
Duncan. "Let me take the baby and you carry my
bundle, Jed."

Fifteen minutes later they reached the battered
old dock and Jed reached beneath it and drew out
Hovey's rowboat. As he did this two things happened: the moon peeped out from behind its cloud

and the baby opened its mouth and let out a wail that could have been heard in Roxbury. They stared at one another in blank astonishment. Then with a little cry Ben jumped down into the boat, placed the two-year-old baby on its floor, grabbed the oars, and heedless of noise slid them into their locks. At the same time Mrs. Duncan jumped into the boat with the baby and sat down. Jed threw after her the bundle of clothes that he carried.

In spite of their haste and panic Mrs. Duncan looked up at Jed on the dock and smiled. "Thank you, Jed," she said. "I do hope we meet again."

Now there were footsteps running across rough ground toward them, and a second later a musket was fired warningly into the air. But as Jed gave the row boat a shove that sent it far out into the river the moon helped them by disappearing again. Darkness closed around the boat until it could no longer be seen from the shore.

It was too late to run away. Jed lowered himself into the icy water, taking care not to make a sound, and swam under the splintery boards. Hanging onto a pile he stayed there, his teeth chattering with cold, while two sentries searched the shore. It was a long time before they gave up and went away, and a longer time before Jed dared to leave his hiding place. Going home he had to dodge redcoats all over again, street by street, until his nerves were ragged.

It was nearly dawn when he lay down on his bench at the printing shop. He was cold, hungry and nearly exhausted. But he had helped. He had done a night's good work. He thought that Major Duncan, his red-haired friend, might be proud of him.

"And tomorrow," he decided, just before falling asleep, "tomorrow I'll try to find out where Mr. Box goes at night."

15

❦ When Jed left the printing shop to follow Mr. Box it had begun to snow again. Autumn had turned into winter. For weeks smallpox had swept through Boston, and hundreds of people had died. General Gage had been called back to England and General Howe had taken his place. Life went on, but there was little to report to Ben when he came to see Jed. It was too cold for fighting. It was hard enough just to stay alive.

He had been following Mr. Box for a long time now and still he did not know Mr. Box's secret—if he had one. So far as Jed knew his master had not gone out at night again, but once a week he would leave the shop by daylight, always with a package under one arm, and always he walked across town to a mansion in the North End. He would go into this house, remain there for half an hour and then walk home again without the package.

Certainly there was nothing wrong with this. Mr. Box was a printer and he was plainly delivering work that he had finished. The people who lived in the house were named Wentworth. They were Tories, but nearly everyone left in Boston town was a Tory. Who else would need printing done?

Yet still Jed felt compelled to follow him. Once there had been no secrets at all between them, but now Mr. Box was silent about his work. The room upstairs was always locked. He never asked Jed to deliver work for him but always went himself.

Glancing up at the bleak gray sky Jed thought what a long winter it was this year. It was December and nothing had happened. The rebels hadn't set fire to Boston and the redcoats hadn't attacked. No one had the energy any longer even to hope for fighting. The people Jed passed in the street were thin and white and pinched-looking. Even so, they were the lucky ones, he guessed, because at least they were still alive and not dead from the smallpox. He wondered how the rebels outside of Boston were faring. The snow was just as deep and cold there, and food divided among an army could never be enough.

He shivered from the cold in spite of the warm

clothes Mr. Box had given him. He'd had a mug of
goldenrod tea only a few minutes ago, but it seemed
that when a person was hungry there was no way to
keep warm. He pulled his knitted muffler across his
chin and tried to shrink into his clothes. The snow
stung his cheeks like needles.

It looked as though Mr. Box was heading for the
same house again. He was crossing the drawbridge
into the North End, and Jed quickened his steps so
he wouldn't lose him. He hated walking through
Boston now. It wasn't just the cold; it was the way
the town looked, with its trees cut down, its fences
and barns gone, and windows and doors missing from
empty houses. Anything that could be burned as firewood was disappearing because people had nothing
else to burn. The North Church had been torn down
and its boards used for fires to keep the soldiers warm.
The old Governor Winthrop house that had stood
for a hundred and forty-five years was gone. The
Liberty Tree had been cut, too—Jed had walked out
toward the gates to see it axed. Still people were
freezing, though, and still the winter dragged along.

Mr. Box was crossing North Square now, and
turning up Princess Street. At the corner of Salem
Jed held back, because the Wentworth house was in
sight. He watched Mr. Box knock at the door and
enter. The door swung shut behind him.

There seemed no point in waiting. Jed turned
and walked quickly back toward Water Street, at
last breaking into a run to keep warm. He entered the

shop and threw his jacket over the bench. As he turned away from the bench he spied a scrap of paper lying on the floor at the bottom of the stairs. He walked over and picked it up.

As he glanced at it his mouth dropped open. "Good heavens!" he gasped, astonished at his carelessness, for this was the American money that Ben Wheeler had given him in the summer, the bill printed by Paul Revere himself at Watertown. He was horrified to find it here on the floor. He thought of how by accident Mr. Box might have entered the shop first and found the bill. It would not have been easy to explain its presence here. A piece of rebel money in Boston town! He would not have been able to explain it at all.

There had to be a hole in his pocket. . . . He stuck his fingers inside and turned the cloth inside out. To his amazement the bill that Ben had given him fell from his pocket to the floor. It had been there all the time. This was a second American bill he had found.

How had it gotten here? Jed knelt beside the place where he had discovered it. He had found it just under the bottom step—and no one went up or down these stairs except Mr. Box. What was Mr. Box doing with a rebel bill?

Breathlessly Jed took the two bills to the window and laid them on the bench, side by side. He knelt and examined them in the light. They looked alike. They were printed on the same cardboard, and were the same size. Both were framed in a square border of scripts and flourishes. Both had been printed on copper plates—he could tell this by the clear print. Each was an eight-dollar bill. He spelled out the words printed on Ben's money:

> This Bill entitles the
> Bearer to receive
> EIGHT Spanish milled
> DOLLARS, or the
> Value thereof, in *Gold*
> or *Silver*, according to
> the Resolution of the
> CONGRESS, held at
> Philadelphia, the 10th of
> May, 1775. VLLL DOLL.

To the left of these words was a circle with Latin words printed inside its band. The words were *"Majora minoribus consonant."*

He turned to the bill he had just found and stared at it, his heart beating fast. It was very strange, Mr. Box's dropping a rebel bill here, he thought. Carefully he studied each word on Mr. Box's bill. There had to be something—some small, overlooked difference—if what he suspected was true.

"Ah," he gasped, suddenly finding the difference. It lay in the Latin words inside the circle: instead of *"Majora minoribus consonant"* Mr. Box's bill had the words *"Mahora minabus consanant"*—but if both had been printed from Mr. Revere's plate the words should have been the same. Only a trained eye would notice the mistake in spelling, but Jed had lived with Mr. Box for a year. He also knew that Ben's bill was a true bill, coming straight from the rebel side.

As he heard Mr. Box stamp his feet outside the door he hastily stuffed the two bills in his pocket. His master walked in, saying cheerfully, "Well, m'boy, just see what I've brought back with me." He brought a small ham from under his cloak and held it up to the light.

It had been months since Jed had seen a ham, but his mind was on the two bills. "That's wonderful," he said politely.

"I expected more enthusiasm than that. Never mind, we'll dine well tonight. Have we enough wood to cook it?"

Jed nodded. "The last branch of the cherry tree."

Mr. Box nodded and walked up the stairs to his printing room.

Jed watched him go. He was almost certain that the bill he had found on the floor was a counterfeit— and Mr. Box had been a counterfeiter; he knew that well enough. But if he was printing false rebel bills in his room upstairs what good could it do him when he lived inside Boston? He could not spend them here. What could be the purpose of it?

Jed shook his head. Bringing out the two bills

again, he studied them wonderingly until he thought
he would go blind from staring at them. He knew
he was going to have to find a way to get into the
room upstairs. He knew he had to find out the reason
behind Mr. Box's printing counterfeit bills again.

It was two days before Mr. Box announced that
he was going out again. "I've run out of copper,
m'boy," he said. "No need for you to go. I need a
breath of fresh air."

Jed nodded. He was just back from the Widow
Muffet's, where he had chopped wood for an hour.
He had had enough fresh air for the day. He watched
Mr. Box leave, and then he went to the window and
watched until Mr. Box disappeared from sight. It had
begun to snow again. He doubted if Mr. Box would
be gone long. It gave Jed very little time—and everything depended on whether Mr. Box had taken the
key to the room with him.

He tiptoed up the stairs and into Mr. Box's bedroom. Of course the key no longer lay on the table
beside the bed; that had been a trick to test him when
he first came to live here. There was not much furniture in the room. He opened the chest that held Mr.
Box's clothes, and then the desk where Mr. Box kept
his accounts. He found the key at last under the
pillow on the bed.

It had been months since he had gone into this
upstairs printing room—since the day Mr. Box was
released from prison and they had walked home to-

gether. But in this room he had learned to read, tracing words with a finger while Mr. Box worked over his press. In this room he had learned that Mr. Box's real trade was printing counterfeit money, and from maps laid across the table he had learned the shape of Boston town and Roxbury and Dorchester and Cambridge. Those had been good days.

It looked no different now—less tidy, perhaps, because Hovey was no longer here to clear it. At one end of the long table lay copper plates and tools and inks for engraving. At the other end sat the press, and a pile of paper. A dozen candles and two betty lamps rested in the center of the table. It was hard to get enough bright light for such fine work. The two windows in the room were shuttered and barred. It was no wonder that Mr. Box's eyes were so often red-rimmed and puffy in the morning.

Jed hesitated, wanting to leave, wanting to believe that everything was the same and that Mr. Box was printing honest handbills for the people left in Boston town. Yet from the look of things he knew that it was money Mr. Box was printing. There were no handbills lying around; there was no wood for cutting wood blocks. There were only the small plates and small tools. Jed drew closer to the table. He lit a candle and held it over the copper engraving plate nearest him.

And there it was—the engraving plate on which Mr. Box had carved all the words for the American eight-dollar bill Jed had found downstairs. Here, too,

were the misspelled Latin words. There was no doubt
that Mr. Box was printing counterfeit bills in this
room.

But not British bills; American ones this time—
bills put out by the Continental Congress.

But why American bills? Why not British?

A sheet of white paper caught his eye. It had
been tucked under a heavy candlestick to keep it
from blowing away. He picked it up, opened it and
read:

MR. TITHERMING BOX:
> *No later than March 1st you will deliver to
> us the following:*

one engraved plate for the printing of ½-dollar
                              Continental bills

one engraved plate for the printing of 20-dollar
                              Continental bills

one engraved plate for the printing of 8-dollar
                              Continental bills

one engraved plate for the printing of 10-dollar
                              Continental bills

> *Kindly deliver same—all carefully rendered
> to deceive the eye of the enemy—to M. Went-
> worth, Esquire, of Salem street.*
>> Signed,
>>> MAJOR E. LAWES
>>> *aide to General Burgoyne*

Jed gasped. To deceive the eye of the enemy—and signed by a British army officer! He fell back into a chair and chewed a fingernail as he thought of it. He realized that Mr. Box wasn't printing these bills just for himself as he had always done before. He wasn't trying to fool the British as he had always done before, either. No, he was working hand in glove with the British—openly, and without any fear of being arrested. The British *wanted* Mr. Box to print counterfeit bills. That meant it had to be harmful to the Americans. It had to be.

He sat there and remembered Mr. Box in jail, dirty and hungry. He'd said, "I'll be out of this jail before a month is over, Jed." And months later, like a miracle, Mr. Box had been freed and his press returned to him. It had seemed a little strange—certainly nobody else had been so lucky. "The important thing to remember," he'd told Jed when they met again, "is always to land on your feet—like a cat, m'boy. No bruises, no hurts. You can learn a lot from a cat."

Then this was the reason Mr. Box had been freed from prison—he had made a deal with the British. They wanted a printer to make false American bills, and he had wanted his freedom. The British were making an honest criminal of Mr. Box and at the same time a traitor of him to the Americans.

"Oh Mr. Box," whispered Jed, with tears in his eyes. He wished he had never come up here. He wished Mr. Box had never dropped that bill on the floor. He thought of all the rebel Americans in prison for what they believed in. He didn't think Mr. Box believed in anything except landing on his feet. Yet he knew he could never betray Mr. Box. This was a secret that had to remain a secret.

Carefully he wiped away the candle wax that had dropped on the table. He placed the candlestick and the engraving plates where he had found them, snuffed out the candle and sadly locked the door behind him.

16

❧ It was a crisp, cold January night when Jed started home from the *Ship's Mermaid*. The Widow Muffet had kept him late, but he didn't mind, for she had given him a shilling and a bowl of hotchpotch with slivers of meat in it. He didn't know where she had found the meat or what kind it was. People were eating such strange things these days that it was better not to ask.

The streets were nearly empty, for it was well past eight o'clock and bitterly cold. Faneuil Hall was brightly lighted, and as he passed it he could hear laughter from inside. He guessed the British were putting on another play to entertain themselves, and he wondered what the Americans were doing in their camps. He had begun to notice that Ben spoke less and less of the army outside of Boston. He supposed it meant they were having their troubles, too. Winter was a terrible time to be a soldier.

He had gone several blocks beyond Faneuil Hall when he realized that he was being followed. He would not have noticed it if the streets were not deserted. He had been dimly aware for some time of footsteps behind him on the cobbles, but what alarmed him was that when he stopped at a street corner the footsteps stopped, too. This was when it occurred to him that someone might be following him deliberately.

He felt a touch of fear. He remembered that he had only yesterday walked past Fort Hill to count the cannons again. Perhaps someone had noticed how often he hung around the batteries. Or perhaps Ben had been followed last week, when he came to the printing shop and tapped on the window after curfew. Perhaps the British had known about them both for some time, and had been following Jed for days. He could feel cold sweat on the back of his neck.

Reaching a decision, he ducked into the first alley he passed, and pressed himself against the wall. He heard the boots come abreast of him and saw a tall, bulkily dressed man walk by. It was no one he knew. The boots continued past the alley and Jed relaxed. Then he stiffened as the boots slowed and

stopped. He heard them coming back and he closed
his eyes and prayed he couldn't be seen. When he
opened his eyes again the man was standing beside
him. "I didn't mean to frighten you," he said in a low
voice.

Jed would have known that voice anywhere—
it belonged to the red-haired major. "Major Duncan!" he gasped weakly.

"Aye, it's me, Jed," the man said.

"But here—in Boston town?"

"I've been here before, lad, and will doubtless
come again."

Jed said in horror, "But if they should see you!"

The major chuckled. "They've seen me but I
doubt if even you would recognize me, Jed. I'm
dressed like a fisherman and my hair is no longer red
and I reek of fish and I've a pass signed by a British
officer. But never mind—I've only one last errand
and then I'll be leaving town."

"Do you need my help for it?" asked Jed hopefully.

"No, only your ear, for my last errand is to
thank you for helping my wife and children out of
Boston. I was down in New York when her message
came out, saying she was in danger, and it was Ben
and his father who decided what to do."

Jed felt his cheeks go scarlet and he was glad the
major couldn't see him. "Oh, it was nothing, sir.
Really. I was glad to help."

"My wife tells me you're quite a lad, with a

good head on your shoulders. It couldn't have been done without you. She was very uneasy until Ben reported you reached home safely that night."

"Yes, sir, I got away all right."

"By hiding in the water. A rather cold solution, I'd say."

Jed smiled. "Yes, it was."

"We're both of us in your debt, Jed." He added in a lower voice, "You may not see Ben this week. Is there anything to report?"

Jed shook his head. "No—nothing, sir. Not really." He hesitated, wondering if he could draw information from the major without giving Mr. Box away. "It's just——"

"Yes?"

"It's just—I overheard redcoats talking at the tavern," he lied. "It was something about the British printing false American money—counterfeit bills, that is. Would that be important? If it's true," he added hastily.

"Important?" repeated the major. "Jed, it would be of deadly importance. It would be terrible."

"It would?" said Jed with a sinking heart.

"Of course—Good heavens, let us hope you heard wrong!"

"It really would harm the American side?"

"Very much so."

Jed shook his head. "I don't understand."

The major was silent a moment, thinking. "Let me explain it this way, Jed. It's like adding water to a thick, rich stew. A little water isn't noticed; a bit more thins the stew; but if you add a great deal of water it ruins the stew. You have to throw it out. It's worthless."

Jed frowned. "Yes, but——"

"It's like this: When a government issues paper money it plans the amount carefully. Not too much, not too little; just enough to keep business thick and bubbling. But if you add thousands of dollars of counterfeit money it dilutes the mixture, Jed—just like stew. It ruins the government and you have to throw it out."

Jed whistled faintly.

"Because paper money is only a promise," added the major seriously. "It's a promise, and if there are too many promises none of them can be kept. Then the paper money becomes worthless. It won't buy anything. Nobody respects it any longer. Nobody respects the government that put it out."

"Oh," said Jed in a sad, small voice.

"A devilish trick, as you can see. So if you hear anything again, Jed, try to find out more. It would be the most important thing you could do to help."

"Yes," Jed said in a dull voice. With all his heart he longed to tell the major that he had seen the bills and that it was Mr. Box who was making them. But he couldn't. Mr. Box had been kind to him; Mr. Box was the first friend he'd ever had. Mr. Box had rescued him from Silas Clark's smithy, and taught him to read, and given him warm clothes and affection. How could he betray him?

"I've got to be going," the major said. "Take

care of yourself now, lad, and my thanks again." As abruptly as he had come into the alley he was gone.

When the sound of the major's boots had died away Jed left the alley, too, and went home to Mr. Box.

Jed thought about the major's words for three days, and then out of desperation decided he had to speak to Mr. Box. It was a reckless decision, but it was his only hope. He could never betray his master. . . . Perhaps there was some way to change him.

They dined that night on dried codfish, and as usual Mr. Box made a face at it. He said wearily, "Remind me never to eat dried codfish again when this miserable siege is over. *Never*."

"You still think the British will win?" asked Jed.

"Of course! Don't talk nonsense."

"They've not done very well yet, sir. If they don't do something soon they'll be starved out of Boston or driven into the sea by the Americans."

Mr. Box looked at him in surprise. "My dear Jed," he said, "the English always win. It's true that someday they may lose but not to a bunch of farmers and candlestick makers and tavern keepers! As for the Americans starving us out"—he pointed his fork at Jed—"mark my words, the ships will be coming in soon with food and more soldiers from England. And then, m'boy—" He snapped his fingers. "So much for your troublemakers!"

"It doesn't scare you, sir, that thirteen colonies

have declared war on England now? And that England's ships are being captured at sea by American privateers, which is why so few of them reach Boston?"

Mr. Box put down his fork and stared at Jed. "Where do you hear such wild stories, m'boy? What are you up to?"

Jed drew from his pocket the two bills and laid them on the table. He said in a voice that was bolder than he felt, "I know what you're printing upstairs, Mr. Box. You dropped one of these on the floor not long ago."

Mr. Box glanced at the two bills. "And may I ask how you knew they're counterfeit? Have I trained you that well, m'boy?"

"Only one of them is counterfeit," replied Jed.

Mr. Box said dryly, "You're hurting my feelings, Jed. I rather fancied my bills to be perfect copies. You took the key from under my pillow, didn't you? I thought things looked different in the room upstairs."

Jed gasped, "Yes, sir."

Mr. Box regarded him thoughtfully. "I bought you from Silas Clark because you were a bright boy, Jed. You'll make me sorry yet, I fear." He sighed. "Yes, I'm back at the old trade, and hanged if I know why I didn't tell you so, but you've such a regard for those fools who want to fight the Crown!"

"Yes, sir, I have," said Jed doggedly.

"Why?"

Jed hesitated. "Because they fight to be free. Because they believe that men are born equal. And because I can never forget the sound of the bells I heard at Concord."

Mr. Box shook his head sadly. "There's no such thing as freedom in this world, m'boy. Maybe in the next world, but not in this one. Never has been and never will."

Jed said breathlessly, "But there could be, couldn't there? Just one country without a king, where *people* decide on the laws and have some rights?"

Mr. Box smiled bitterly. "A dream, Jed—a dream that can never come true. There will always be kings, and kings don't want men to be free. A year from now your heroes will all be in jail or hanged by the king they dare to fight."

Jed said hotly, "And you're helping to put them in that jail by making counterfeit bills for the English!"

Mr. Box said in astonishment, "You'd prefer I had stayed in prison? Yes, I made a bargain with them —you don't think they let men go free out of kindness, do you? I told you before, Jed, the only important thing for people like you and me is to land on our feet."

Jed said with an angry sob, "Why?"

"Why, because you and I are poor people, Jed. We have no rights and no hope of bettering ourselves. Does anybody care what happens to us? Was there anybody to help you when you were thrown onto a ship and kidnapped? Of course not."

"Then how can you believe in the cause of the English?" asked Jed.

"Believe in the English?" Mr. Box looked shocked. "Good heavens, m'boy, you think I *believe* in them? You think I like that fat and foolish king who sits on the throne? I despise him—but don't you understand he's rich and he's powerful?"

Jed said sadly, "You don't believe in anything, then."

Mr. Box smiled. "Why yes—I believe in Titherming Box, m'boy. Nothing else. And since you're bound out to Titherming Box for another four and a half years it might be wise of you to think as I do and stay out of trouble."

"Yes, sir," said Jed forlornly.

Mr. Box said in a kinder voice, "You're young, Jed, and you think too much. Wars come and go. The important thing is to stay alive. Long after that General Washington of yours is hanged, Titherming Box will still be here on Water Street printing whatever needs to be printed. And that, m'boy, is all that matters."

All that matters to *you*, thought Jed, and gave up his arguing and went to fetch the bread pudding to the table.

17

❧ By February Boston was surrounded by ice instead of water. She was no longer an island, for the ice was frozen hard enough to hold an army, and as the ice grew stronger the people in Boston grew more and more afraid of an attack. Every night at the Widow Muffet's the rumors that Jed heard grew wilder, but he dutifully reported them to Ben when he saw him. Any rumor heard from a British soldier might turn out to be true.

On the twelfth of February Jed waited for Ben's visit with unusual impatience. Until that day all the rumors he'd overheard at the tavern had concerned the Americans and what they were planning to do. Tonight he had heard something different. When Ben tapped on the window Jed took only a minute to reach the garden. "Ben," he said in a low, excited voice.

"Something new?"

Jed nodded. "Yes. You know the two officers who are billeted at Mrs. Muffet's for the winter? I heard them talking upstairs. The British are marching tomorrow."

"Good heavens—tomorrow?" gasped Ben. "How long ago since you heard this?"

"Only a few hours or I'd have crossed the ice to the house in Cambridge. Of course it may not be true, but they were officers, Ben."

"But did you hear where they're marching?"

"Yes—to Dorchester Heights."

"Dorchester Heights!" Ben's voice sounded bewildered.

Now it was Jed's turn to be bewildered. "Why yes—isn't that where the American army is? The British have heard so. They plan to march there in the morning, take the Americans by surprise and wipe them all out."

"Oh." To Jed's surprise a sound escaped Ben that sounded very much like a giggle. "Oh, Jed, I didn't mean to laugh," said Ben, "but it's funny, all the same. I've never told you where the American army is, in case you were captured, but they're not *there*."

"Really?" gasped Jed with pleased surprise.

"Honest. If it's true and the British do march to Dorchester Heights—but it isn't a joke," he added hastily, "because there are probably sentries posted there, so I must hurry back anyway. But if the British march they'll find nothing. You're sure the officers said Dorchester Heights?"

"Oh yes."

"What regiment do they belong to, do you know?"

"The Royal Fusiliers, I think."

Ben nodded. "The King's own regiment. Funny —it scarcely seems possible, but I'll hurry back and tell the Major." He turned to go and then he came back and laid his hand on Jed's arm. He whispered, "I nearly forgot—I have good news for you. We have cannons across the river now. *Cannon*, Jed— forty-three of them and sixteen mortars!"

"Cannons?" echoed Jed blankly. "But I thought the Americans had none at all."

"They're what were captured from the British at Fort Ticonderoga last summer," whispered Ben, and before Jed could ask him any more Ben had vanished into the darkness again.

Jed tiptoed back into the shop, his mind spinning. The Americans were not on Dorchester Heights, after all. The Americans had cannon now. As he lay down on the bench and pulled the blanket over him he wished he could roam around and see the things Ben saw. It was hard to know so little. But

cannon! Cannon was what any real army needed.
Just one was worth a hundred muskets. Why, you
could place a cannon as far away as Bunker's Hill
and its lead would fall into Boston's North Square.
A cannon could shoot miles, a musket only a few
paces.

He thought drowsily, just before falling asleep,
"I wonder where Fort Ticonderoga is, anyway. . . ."

At dawn the next morning the British redcoats
marched out of Boston to attack Dorchester Heights,
but although Jed listened in suspense, the entire
morning passed without any sound of gunfire.

As the day dragged on, Jed borrowed Mr. Box's
maps, beautifully drawn on oilskin, and laid them out
on the floor of the shop. He had learned to read from
these maps, but he recalled no Fort Ticonderoga, nor
did he find it. At last he went upstairs and knocked
on Mr. Box's door.

"Come in," said Mr. Box, adding dryly, "You
might as well, since you know my business now."

Jed carried in the maps and tried to avoid looking at the copper engraving plates on the table and
the false American bills hung up to dry. "I want to
know where Fort Ticonderoga might be," he said.

His master shot him a quick glance but did not
question him. He must have known very well that
the British had surrendered there in the summer. Perhaps he did not want to start a fresh argument. "It
would be about here," he said, pointing to a blank

space at the corner of the map. "It lies in the colony of New York."

Nearly all of that western side of the map was empty, and Jed said in a puzzled voice, "There? But what do all the blank spaces mean?"

"Forest," said Mr. Box. "Wilderness. Now run along and let me finish my work."

Jed withdrew to spread out the map again downstairs. If Fort Ticonderoga was there, and Boston here . . . Why, there were at least three hundred miles between the two, he thought in astonishment. There had to be some mistake, there was no possible way to move cannon that far. There were no rivers for the cannons to be floated down on barges, and there were no roads. If this map was right, there were only forests—and this was winter. How could cannon be dragged three hundred miles through the snow?

Yet Ben had said they had cannon now, and the cannon came from Fort Ticonderoga. He could not doubt Ben, and yet—how could it be? He had seen the British move a cannon from Fort Hill to Copp's Battery. It had taken dozens of men, stout ropes and a great deal of shouting to mount the cannon on a wagon. Then they had found that one team of horses couldn't pull the weight, and so they had gone off to find more horses. Then a wheel had fallen off and they had called for a wheelwright. In the end they had taken the cannon off the wagon and waited for a barge which had floated the cannon around to Copp's Hill by water. It had taken two days to move that cannon one mile.

But Ben said they had cannon.

A little smile curled the corners of Jed's lips as he thought about it. Perhaps it was a little like the church bells that had been rung in Lexington and Concord and Acton and Bedford, signaling minutemen all over the countryside. Perhaps when people wanted freedom badly enough they made up their own ways of doing things. Perhaps they even did the impossible—not because they were an army but because they were just people—farmers and candlestick makers and tavern keepers, as Mr. Box had called them.

Jed wondered, and was proud.

At dusk, the British soldiers marched back into Boston. They had spent the day tramping over the hills of Dorchester and burning barns and sheds, but they had found no American army. Certainly they looked a little foolish marching back into Boston empty-handed.

Suddenly, during the night of March second, the Americans began to fire their cannons. The first roar woke Jed from a sound sleep and he sat up, rubbing his eyes and shaking his head to clear it. He heard Mr. Box's feet strike the floor upstairs and a moment later he came downstairs carrying a candle. When he spoke Jed couldn't hear him because the cannons were speaking in a louder voice. The house shook, and a pot in the kitchen fell from its hook and rolled on the floor.

Mr. Box's lips continued to move. He came

closer and shouted, "Those are *American* cannon. Is it an attack? We must find out. . . . Get dressed."

Together they hurried out into the street. There was no fear of arrest tonight because the sound of American shooting had brought others out to see, too. Shadowy forms ran past them, and candles were lit in windows. "In here," shouted Mr. Box, tugging at Jed's arm. He pointed to the deserted mansion that Jed called the Potato House because from its garden in the autumn he had dug potatoes. Its doors and windows had been torn off for firewood, and through the gaping door Jed saw that the front staircase had vanished, too. But Mr. Box must have been inside before because he drew Jed to the rear. The back stairs were still standing, and they ran to the second floor and then to the attic.

Crawling to the small fanlight window set into the eaves, they looked out over the roofs of Boston and across the river toward Cambridge. They had an excellent view from this height—too good, thought Jed nervously, hoping no cannon ball would find its way through the window they sat behind. From here there seemed to be cannons everywhere along the American lines, from Cambridge in an arc to the south. It was like watching heat lightning run up and down the horizon: a light would flash, and then would come the roar of thunder and then to the north another flash, another roar. There was no doubt about the Americans' having artillery now.

The British cannons began to return the fire, and

after a while the flashes from the American side came less frequently. "Low on ammunition, probably," said Mr. Box scornfully. "They're just showing off. Certainly there's no sign of any attack. Let's go home."

They went to bed again, but Jed doubted that Mr. Box slept. Certainly he himself didn't, for the English cannons kept firing and once in a while the Americans would answer. Jed lay awake listening to the noise and to the shaking of pans in the kitchen and he was excited about what might happen next. "They can't just be showing off," he reasoned. "The British didn't know they had cannon until tonight. Even if their spies told them so, they couldn't be sure until they heard them. The Americans wouldn't waste ammunition because they don't have much. For a while they didn't have any at all, Ben said so."

The cannons stopped firing before dawn. Heavy-eyed from lack of sleep, Jed crawled out of bed to face another ordinary day. On his way to the widow Muffet's he went out of his way to look around, but little had been damaged by the American cannons. A few fires had broken out, but the British had quickly put them out. He heard a man say in the street, "They may have cannon but they've not learned how to hit anything with 'em!"

After the excitement of the night it was almost unbearable to go back to reality. Reality meant sweeping out the tavern for Mrs. Muffet, and mixing ink for Mr. Box, and trying to build a fire with sawdust and twigs of green wood, and going to bed at curfew.

But that night the American cannons began firing again. Jed sat up, puzzled. After a few minutes Mr. Box stamped down the stairs to stare angrily out of the window. "It's not enough that we're hungry," he said indignantly. "No, they've got to keep us from sleeping, too." Having said this, he stamped angrily up the stairs again. Obviously he did not fear an attack any longer. Jed lay listening to the cannons, but after an hour of this he flung off his blanket and dressed. He wandered through the streets for an hour and at last made his way through the common to the Cambridge side of Boston. He stayed there for a long time, watching the bursts of light from British and American cannon.

The shooting stopped again at dawn.

So far the cannons had robbed Boston only of sleep, but by now sleep was all that mattered. On the third night most of Boston went to bed at sunset, and Jed among them. He closed his eyes, dreamed wild dreams, woke with a jump and then slept again. But when the cannons began firing again he opened his eyes, completely awake, and dressed hastily in warm clothes. He preferred the cannons to silence. He *wanted* them to fire.

This time he made his way to the Dorchester side of Boston, and sat on a wharf at the end of Sea Street. He did not know why he had to be outside. It was true that he felt safer in the open, but the firing puzzled him deeply. There seemed to be no rhyme or reason to it, and he kept trying to understand the plan behind it. He simply could not believe the rebels would waste ammunition so recklessly on what Mr. Box called showing off.

Tonight was worst of all, for tonight the British cannon kept up a steady firing—as if, thought Jed, they had to prove they had more shells. It was bedlam. Jed made himself as small as possible by hugging his knees with his arms and digging his chin into his knees. It was a mild night for March. Boston was well lit by moonlight, but here close to the water the mist was thick and damp. Jed could see no farther than the end of the wharf. Beyond that the fog made a thick white wall.

It must have been a little after ten o'clock when there came a brief lull in the firing. Jed was dozing on the wharf, and the sudden silence startled him more than the noise. He lifted his head, and in those few moments between cannon shots he heard some very strange sounds. He could not have said exactly what they were. The sounds came from across the water, from somewhere beyond the fog, muffled by both the fog and the wind that tried to blow the sounds away. Jed got slowly to his feet and stared out across the water toward Dorchester Heights. He strained his ears to hear more, but as suddenly as the firing had stopped it began again, and Jed was left staring into the pearly mist and trying to think of what the noises reminded him.

Those had been sounds of *work*, he decided, trying desperately to identify them—of things moving out there in the darkness. It was impossible to explain it more clearly because the faint noises had left only an impression, but *something* was going on out there under cover of darkness—yes, and under cover of the cannon's thunder, he realized with growing excitement. Was it possible that he had stumbled on the reason behind the Americans' firing? Was it possible that the Americans were firing only to conceal noise?

He turned his eyes again to the mist that covered the water. He thought he had to be wrong, for over that way lay Dorchester Heights, and the redcoats had marched there less than a month ago and found nothing. No forts, no trenches, no redoubts, no military stores. Nobody could build a fort or make earthworks in the dead of winter, with the ground frozen into rock. It was impossible.

Yet still he stared into the mist, wishing the cannons would stop firing again for a second. He hoped with all his heart that he had heard right, because for that one moment he had been certain that something was happening beyond the fog.

18

When morning came and the mists rolled away Jed found that his ears had not betrayed him. Overnight, the American army had moved to the hills of Dorchester. In the space of twelve hours an empty hill had been turned into a fort. Twenty cannons pointed directly at Boston town, and breastworks had been built to hide thousands of riflemen. The British were in terrible danger.

How had the Americans moved cannon to the hill under the eyes and ears of the enemy? How had they managed to put up breastworks when the ground was frozen solid?

Long afterward Jed heard how the magic had

been accomplished. It had not been easy. It had taken clever planning and three nights of hard work during which American cannons had banged away at the British to keep them from suspecting anything. First had come two hundred and fifty men to cut down trees and build screens of branches behind which men could work. Then, on the second night of the bombardment, hay and straw had been scattered all along the road to Dorchester so that no one in Boston would hear the sound of carts passing. Then had come the cannon, and hundreds of barrels filled with earth and stones to roll down the hills at the enemy if they attacked. Earthworks? There was no way of heaping up the earth for protection, and so breast-works had been built on top of the earth, of sticks tied together into bundles and stuck into wooden frames already made back at camp. These had been put into position on the third night, and the cannon mounted—the cannons from Fort Ticonderoga that Henry Knox, his men and oxen had dragged on sleds through the wilderness of Massachusetts for three hundred miles.

But Jed did not know this then, and it seemed as much like magic to him as it did to the people left in Boston.

When Mr. Box walked out to Sea Street with Jed to stare across the water, his eyes were eager. He rubbed his hands together and said, "Now we'll see some action, m'boy. The British can never allow *this* sort of thing to happen."

"But it's already happened," pointed out Jed.

Mr. Box shook his head. "Not really. Those soldiers over there are no more settled than a mosquito on a nose. They can still be easily brushed away. See? They're still dashing around working and getting organized. Run off to Province House, Jed, and see if the British aren't getting ready to attack."

Jed found a great deal of excitement at Province House. For several hours he watched soldiers lining up, and when they marched down to the wharves he followed them. All morning and well into the afternoon the soldiers filled the docks and were taken out to ships in the harbor. One by one he saw the ships haul off to form a line between Boston and the hills of Dorchester.

Disconsolate, Jed walked down Ship Street to Mrs. Muffet's tavern.

"You're late, Jed," she told him cheerfully. "Hustle along now. The tables need scrubbing, the floor sweeping—and I've got a mug of hot cider for you."

"How can you be so happy when the British are going to attack?" he asked gloomily. "All their ships are lining up out there to attack at first light in the morning."

Mrs. Muffet only laughed. "I'm not a captain's widow for nothing, Jed," she said mysteriously. "Why, I've sailed with my husband to Madagascar and Bombay and Singapore. I've been at sea most of my life, Jed. Good afternoon, Mr. Perry," she said, as the door swung wide. "A glass of mead, is it?" She scurried off to fetch it, leaving Jed with the broom in his hand.

It was dark when she dismissed him at last, giving him a loaf of corn bread to take with him for Mr. Box. "Cheer up, Jed," she told him with a smile. "They'll not be attacking in the morning."

"How do you know?" he asked.

She laughed, and came to stand in the door beside him. "Listen," she told him.

He could hear nothing but a faint, faraway roar that was not familiar to him.

"I've heard that sound before," she said. "Out there beyond the harbor the seas are running wild. I could tell by the sky this afternoon that a bad storm was brewing. That roar is the wind—oh, but this will be a cruel one. Heaven help those at sea tonight!"

When Jed entered the printing shop there were drops of rain on his cheeks. Mr. Box was upstairs. Jed knelt by the window to listen to the patter of rain on the glass. After a time the sound made him sleepy and he pulled a blanket over him and slept. When he awoke in the night it was to hear a chimney brick crash into the street outside the shop. A howling wind was driving the rain against the window and threatening to break the glass. Water was running in under the door.

Jed shivered, thinking of the Americans camped on the heights of Dorchester in a storm like this. Then he remembered that most of the British army had boarded ships that afternoon and must be lying

in hammocks on deck, seasick and frightened by the
pitching, rolling seas. He decided the Americans had
the better of it, for they at least were on land.

Mrs. Muffet was right. When the storm ended
and daylight came the British ships had been scattered
in a dozen directions. Some had lost their anchors and
some their masts. There was no hope of their landing
troops that morning to fight the Americans on Dorchester Heights. They would have to attack another
day.

Mr. Box looked pale that morning, as if he had
not slept well. Instead of going upstairs to work at
his press immediately after breakfast he sat in the
kitchen, his face thoughtful. Once he said with a
sharp laugh, "The weather seems to be on the side of
your friends this week, Jed."

"Aye, that it does," Jed said cheerfully.

"Do you know any of the Americans over
there?" he asked, his eyes watching Jed.

"One or two."

He nodded. "The skies are clearing. I want you
to forget your chores this morning, I want you to
forget Mrs. Muffet. I want you to go and find out
what they're planning at Province House. They've
got to attack today," he added angrily. "They've got
to, or it'll soon be too late."

"Yes, sir," agreed Jed quite happily.

But he brought back little news to satisfy Mr.
Box. One soldier at Province House told him there

were no new orders; another said they were to board ships at noon. Still another told him the generals were having a fight of their own at headquarters. "You don't think anybody wants to march against *them*, do you?" the soldier said, jerking his head toward Dorchester. "They've had two nights and a day to get ready for us. It'll be ten times worse than Breed's Hill—and they tell me we won that fight," he added bitterly.

Hearing this, Mr. Box sighed. "These are difficult days, m'boy," he said. "Difficult days indeed for a man who tries to mind his own business. Those two people you know among the rebels," he said carelessly. "Just who might they be?"

Surprised, Jed said, "Why, one of them is Ben. He's fourteen, sir, and—" Seeing Mr. Box's face fall he added with pride, "and the other is a major, sir."

Mr. Box brightened. "A major, eh?" He beamed at Jed. "I won't ask how you met them, m'boy, but only if you know them well."

Jed said cautiously, "Oh yes, sir, quite well."

Mr. Box nodded and stood up. "Very interesting. Yes, very interesting," he said, and went upstairs.

19

The next day was March seventh. The Americans had occupied the heights of Dorchester for three days and the British had still not attacked. "What on earth is the matter with them?" demanded Mr. Box at breakfast. "This goes beyond belief." He looked, if anything, a little paler. Clearly he was not sleeping well.

Jed said comfortingly, "I heard it said that new troops are due any day now from England, sir." He smiled at his trying to cheer up Mr. Box, but it was easy for him to do. Every day saw the Americans more settled on Dorchester's hills, and at any moment

their cannons could fire on Boston. The town was in
a state of total confusion. No, Jed did not mind com-
forting Mr. Box at all.

"Ha," snorted his master, "they've been saying
that for weeks!" He put down his bread in disgust.
"I'll go myself to Province House this morning,
m'boy. I've done excellent work for the British—
they can jolly well tell me why they haven't marched
against those rebels yet."

When he had gone Jed blew out the tiny fire
that had been kindled to heat their tea. He gave a
glance at the small supply of dried herbs and roots
hanging from the rafters. Their one hope was that
spring was coming, and although there might be no
more food then, somehow when spring came he
thought it would be easier to be hungry. He scoured
the pots with sand, thinking Mr. Box was gone a long
time. He had just put away the birch broom when
the door opened and he looked up to see Mr. Box
standing there. For a moment Jed thought he was
sick.

"Are you all right?" he cried, running to help
him. "Mr. Box, what's the matter?"

His master stood in the doorway looking as if
he had received a great shock. "Jed," he gasped.

Jed took him by the arm and led him to the
bench. "What is it, sir?"

Mr. Box gave a strange, wild laugh. "I have just
been informed—I have just been told—" He looked
up at Jed in surprise. "I couldn't believe my ears."

"What, sir?"

He said in a faint, wondering voice, "The British aren't going to attack the rebels at all!"

"They're not?" gasped Jed.

"On the contrary—" He gave his bitter laugh again. "On the contrary, Jed, they've given orders to evacuate Boston!"

Jed sat down suddenly, his knees weak. "Evacuate?" he echoed.

Mr. Box nodded. "They're pulling out—leaving —quitting Boston town, surrendering it to the rebels. They're not going to attack at all." He shook his head. "I can scarcely believe it."

Jed felt like giving a whoop of joy, but out of consideration for Mr. Box he was silent. Nevertheless, happiness spread through him like a tonic, blotting out hunger and cold and tiredness. Boston town was to be free. It would no longer belong to the Crown. British troops would no longer occupy it. Why, it meant that the Americans had won the town without a shot's being fired!

"It comes as a bit of a shock to me," explained Mr. Box. "They knew yesterday they were going to evacuate—yesterday!" He jumped to his feet angrily. "And not a thought to the people here who depend upon them!"

Jed said in astonishment, "You can't mean they're going to leave all the Tories behind?"

"No, no, not really," he said absently, beginning to pace the room. "That is—they'll take any Tories who want to go. But it's so unfair," he complained, stopping in his tracks. "Anyone going with them has to leave everything behind—everything! There won't be room aboard the ships for furniture or trunks or printing presses. And where are they going to take everyone? To Halifax."

"Halifax!" exclaimed Jed.

"Aye—Halifax."

"Will you—that is, will we be going?" asked Jed dazedly.

"As well go to Timbuctoo!" said Mr. Box in an outraged voice. "What am I to do in Halifax without a printing press? It's my trade—without it I'd starve. Yes, Halifax is where we'll be going unless the British get a better idea. What have we to eat or drink, Jed? This lack of food dulls my wits. Tea?"

"I'll make some," Jed said, and hurried away to use up still more of their precious kindling and tea. He brought Mr. Box a mug of it and stood and watched him drink it.

"Ah yes," he said, nodding. "This helps. Yes, Jed, m'boy, this helps a great deal." He stood up and handed him the emptied mug. "For a few moments there the shock of this unhinged me." He tapped his brow with a finger. "Wits are all we can rely on, you and I. A little thinking goes a long way—I believe I'll go out now."

"Again, sir?"

Mr. Box nodded. "Again, yes, but I'll be back soon." Winding his muffler about his throat, he closed the door behind him.

Jed waited only a moment and then he snatched

up his jacket and followed. He did not try to catch up with Mr. Box because he realized he wanted to be alone; he trailed behind, watching him closely in fear the shock might have been too much for him. At first he thought his master was bound for Province House again, but he veered toward the Wentworth mansion on Salem Street, the house to which he had delivered his counterfeit bills and plates for making them. Once there, he began acting very strangely.

First he walked slowly past the house, giving it quick, secret glances. Then he walked back at a fast pace, scarcely glancing toward it at all, and suddenly ducked behind a tree where he stood at least five minutes watching the house. After that he strolled casually to the rear of the mansion and disappeared.

Curious, Jed stole around to the lane that ran behind the house and crept up toward it from the rear. Kneeling behind a low stone wall he saw Mr. Box take out a knife and gently force open a rear window. A minute later he climbed through it into the house.

This was so surprising to Jed that he scarcely had time to wonder what Mr. Box was up to. He knew only that Mr. Box was adding another crime to his list, and he watched with his heart in his mouth lest his master be caught. But he need not have worried. A minute later Mr. Box appeared at the window and tossed out a large leather bag. He followed it feet first, closed the window carefully behind him, picked up the leather bag and walked away, leaving Jed

flabbergasted at his coolness. A robbery in broad daylight—and what could he have taken from that
house?

Now it was Jed who worried about being seen,
and he slipped away and raced back to the printing
shop, anxious to arrive there before his master did.
But it was a full hour before Mr. Box returned, and
to Jed's surprise he did not carry the leather bag with
him. There was no sign of it at all. Instead he brought
a huge old wheelbarrow which he trundled right into
the shop with him. "Give me a hand, will you,
m'boy?" he said cheerfully. "I want to load my press
on this."

Jed bit back a thousand questions and said nothing. He helped Mr. Box carry the press down the
narrow stairs and place it on the barrow. "That
large piece of oilskin will cover it nicely," said Mr.
Box. "Where might it be, Jed?"

It was discovered in the kitchen and Mr. Box
lovingly wrapped his press in it. "What are you going to do with it?" Jed asked at last, completely
puzzled.

"Oh, nothing in particular," said Mr. Box
vaguely. "Just want it handy, m'boy. Open the
kitchen door for me, will you? I want to wheel it
into the garden."

"You're going to leave your printing press outside?" gasped Jed. "But it may rain. Someone may
steal it."

"Oh, I'll keep an eye on it," he said.

The next morning the press was gone from the yard, but when Jed ran upstairs to tell Mr. Box he did not seem surprised. Instead he looked rather embarrassed.

"Ah yes, m'boy," he said, nodding. "It's all right —I know where it is, you see. I hid it last night."

"*Hid* it?" gasped Jed.

"Safer that way," said Mr. Box firmly. "If they won't let me take my press to Halifax it's better off in a safe place. No need for you to worry about it, m'boy."

Jed asked no more questions. Mr. Box had hidden the leather bag somewhere, and now he had hidden away his press. Obviously he was making plans. Jed wondered what on earth they could be.

But if Mr. Box was acting strangely these days so was everyone else, for Boston was in a state of confusion and panic. At Province House the chimneys spewed smoke day and night as British officers burned important papers they couldn't take with them. The harbor was black with British ships and sloops. Even fishing boats had been brought in to carry troops away. The streets of Boston were filled with trunks and furniture—Tory families had carried them out, only to abandon them there when they discovered that nothing so big could be taken to Halifax. People wept in the streets at leaving Boston, and wept at the wharves before they were rowed out to the crowded ships. British soldiers roamed the town, breaking into shops and looting houses. The streets were scarcely safe these days and the widow Muffet closed and locked her tavern doors until the evacuation was finished. "I'll not open until *they're* gone and the Americans are here," she said with a sniff.

At last Jed could bear the suspense no longer. At breakfast on the fifteenth of March he looked squarely at Mr. Box and said, "Mr. Box, what ship will we be sailing on? Just when are we to leave with the Tories and the British soldiers?"

Mr. Box looked astonished. "Good heavens, what makes you think we're going, m'boy?"

Jed's mouth dropped. "We're not?"

Mr. Box shook his head. "I told you I've no desire to go to Halifax. As for leaving behind my printing press—why, it's the oldest friend I have. I'd as well leave behind a leg or an arm. No, Jed," he said, leaning back comfortably, "I've decided we've had enough of war and of Boston. I've been thinking you and I would do well to move on. To western Massachusetts, I'm thinking—to find some pretty little village without a printing shop, a place where we're not known. I've always wanted to become an honest printer. Perhaps I'll even make some engravings for you—a picture of the Battle of Breed's Hill, Jed. How would you like that?"

"It sounds wonderful," sighed Jed. "But you know it's impossible," he added bluntly.

"Impossible? Nothing is impossible," said Mr. Box.

Jed said evenly, "There are Americans all around Boston, Mr. Box. They won't let you walk through their lines. They won't be letting anyone leave Boston for months. And you can't stay here with *them*, Mr. Box—they'll find out what you've been doing and they'll put you in jail."

"Why yes, they'd soon find out about me," agreed Mr. Box cheerfully. "That's why I plan to go to them first and tell them. Isn't that what any man does when he turns over a new leaf? He confesses his crimes. And that, m'boy, is what I shall do as soon as the Americans march into Boston."

Jed gaped at him in horror, "You're going to tell them you've been making counterfeit American bills for the British? Mr. Box, they'll hang you as a traitor!"

Mr. Box was beaming. "Oh, I think not, Jed. I think I may even wangle a pass from them through the American lines. A pass for you and me, Jed—and once through their lines we'll have the pick of the colonies for our new home."

"But Mr. Box——"

"Because," he said firmly, "I won't be going to the Americans empty-handed, m'boy. I shall have something of value to offer them. Or rather *you* will have something to offer them—for when the Americans come in I am going to send you to them—and this, m'boy, is what you are going to say . . ."

20

❧ On Sunday, March seventeenth, the last of the British soldiers marched to the wharves to quit Boston town forever, and a few hours later American troops marched in. The next morning Mr. Box ordered Jed to dress in clean linen, comb his hair and wash behind his ears. When this had been done he inspected him critically. "Very well, you'll do," he said. "Good luck to you, m'boy. You remember what you're to tell them?"

Jed nodded. "Yes, sir."

He set out with a feeling of excitement because it was the Americans who were at Province House this time. Shyly he asked at the door if Major Duncan was in Boston yet.

"Aye, he's right here," said the sentry.

"I'd like to see him," Jed said hopefully.

"Well, he's a busy man, son. Come back in a week or two."

A corporal standing nearby said, "Nay, John, you know the major's got some mighty strange friends. You'd better not be hasty."

The sentry gave Jed a second glance. "He's a bit young to be one of Duncan's spies, isn't he?" He shrugged. "Well, tell me your name, son, and I'll send it in. Don't get your hopes up, though."

"Jed Crane," he told him.

A few minutes later the sentry came back wearing a puzzled look. "Blow me down if he doesn't want to see you," he said, and jerking his head toward the front door he said, "Don't keep him waiting."

Jed was shown down a hall and into a room where the red-haired major sat behind a desk. He looked up when Jed walked in, and gave him a grin. "Well, lad, you've come to welcome me back to Boston, have you?"

"That's not exactly why I came," said Jed truthfully, "but you know I'm glad you're here. It's wonderful."

"Aye, that it is," sighed Major Duncan. "But sit down and tell me why you did come, lad."

Jed perched on the edge of a chair, saying, "I came to ask if you're still interested in the counterfeit American money that was being made here in Boston."

The major's eyes widened. "Interested!" he repeated. "Jed, it's hurting us so badly we'd give anything for news of who's making it, and where."

Jed said carefully, "Would you give a safe-conduct pass through the American lines to the man who printed that money—if he turned over to you fifty-thousand pounds of counterfeit American bills?"

Major Duncan's eyes narrowed. He said softly, "One pass for fifty thousand pounds of false bills—it's very tempting, Jed." He looked at him. "You know this man?"

He nodded. "Yes, sir."

The major said grimly, "Of course he ought to be clapped into jail or hung—you know that. Still," he added with a sigh, "to keep fifty thousand pounds of the false stuff from being circulated through the colonies is worth something. It's worth a great deal. Who is he, Jed?"

"My master, sir—Titherming Box of Water Street." He brought a bill from his pocket and laid it on the desk. "He sent one of the bills along to show you."

The major took it and fingered it and held it up to the light. He whistled. "This Mr. Box of yours is an artist, Jed. This is no makeshift bill. I only wish it were. Can you tell the difference?"

"The Latin words on the back are spelled wrong," Jed said. "But I didn't tell him so."

The major flashed him a quick smile. "Good boy." He sat back and stared at the bill. "And he has fifty thousand pounds' worth like this?"

Jed nodded. "Yes, sir. He made them for the British and then he stole them back from the British the day he found out they were going to evacuate Boston. I saw him steal them, sir. I only wish I'd followed him home. He hid the leather bag somewhere along the way but I don't know where. All I know is that when he got back to the shop he didn't have the leather bag, and the money is inside that bag."

"I see," said the major thoughtfully. "And what will he do with this pass he wants?"

"He plans to go west to some small town and forget the war."

The major nodded. "Do you trust him, Jed?"

Jed hesitated. "I don't know," he said honestly. "I want to trust him but I don't know, sir."

"He bends with the wind?" said the major dryly. "We have enough of those, Jed. You know I could have him arrested within the hour and he could make no more bills then."

Jed nodded. "That's what I told him, sir."

"And what did he say?"

Jed flushed. "He said you couldn't risk losing the fifty thousand pounds of counterfeit bills, sir. He said you don't know where they are, or who might find them and spend them."

The major sighed. "He's quite right, Jed. I said

we'd give anything to capture them." He reached for his cap. "Let's go and talk to him, Jed." He stood up and called, "Jacoby—Morse—fall in; we're off to Water Street." Two soldiers appeared from nowhere, and they walked out of Province House together.

The printing shop was dark because it never received the morning sun. The shabby uniforms of the American soldiers looked dark, too, after the bright scarlet of the British. There was only one sound in the room, the scraping of the major's pen as he wrote out a safe-conduct pass for Jed and Mr. Box. When he had finished he sprinkled it with sand and gave it to Mr. Box, saying coldly, "This seals our part of the bargain, Box. The rest is up to you."

"Yes, indeed," said Mr. Box cheerfully. "The fifty thousand pounds are hidden not far from here. Shall we go?"

"After you," said the major firmly. His two soldiers fell in beside Mr. Box—clearly they were not going to risk losing him—and Jed joined the major in the rear. They walked several streets to the west until they came to the empty house from whose attic they had watched the first American bombardment. "The money is hidden in here," explained Mr. Box, and they picked their way over the frozen ground to the rear door. "Take care—the British soldiers have been here and two steps are missing."

He led them through the kitchen and up a nar-

row staircase to the second floor. Here there was a
wide hall cutting the house in half, with large, square
rooms on either side. Mr. Box led them into the front
room. Walking to its fireplace he stooped, reached
inside and up, and from the chimney drew out the
leather bag he had stolen from the mansion on Salem
Street. With a little bow he gave it to the major.
"This is what you wanted, I believe."

The major eagerly opened the bag.

"It's stuffed with money," gasped one of his
soldiers.

"Counterfeit money," the major reminded him.
"Begin counting, Jacoby."

But Jed was watching Mr. Box. He saw his master back up to the fireplace and stealthily, with one
hand, reach up inside the chimney again. He did this
without turning his back upon the major and without
any change in his smile. What he took from the
chimney was small enough to put into his pocket but
Jed noticed that it was heavy enough to make the
pocket sag. "Well, Major?" said Mr. Box cheerfully.

The major was counting and only shook his
head impatiently. Mr. Box gave each of the soldiers
a faint smile, strolled carelessly toward the door,
looked back once and then vanished.

Jed scowled at the door suspiciously, waiting for
Mr. Box to reappear. When nothing happened he
glanced at the major, but Mr. Box's disappearance
had gone unnoticed. Jed looked to the door again. He
could guess what Mr. Box had taken from the chim-

ney and put into his pocket, and he had a sinking
feeling that Mr. Box was not going to come back.

Jed tiptoed from the room and down the hall.
His ears were keen enough to hear the squeak of
wood in the bottom stair. He reached the steps just
in time to see Mr. Box's boots disappear from sight.
Quietly Jed slipped down the stairs to follow him out
into the yard. When Jed called to him, his master
was just putting one leg over a stone wall in the
potato garden behind the house.

"Mr. Box," Jed called in a high voice. "Mr. Box,
where are you going?"

His master stopped and slowly turned his head.
"Why, I'm just going for a little walk, m'boy," he
called gaily.

Jed said accusingly, "It wouldn't be a walk
through the town gates, would it, now that you've
got your pass from Major Duncan?"

"It might," said Mr. Box cheerfully. "I've been
thinking lately that, fond as I am of you, m'boy, it's
time we parted company."

"Then you've forgotten something," Jed told
him angrily. "You've forgotten to give Major Duncan the copper engraving plates that printed those
bills."

Mr. Box's eyes narrowed. "Copper plates?"

"Yes, the plates you just took from the chimney
but didn't give the Major."

Mr. Box lifted one eyebrow and said coolly,
"Perhaps I didn't care to give them to him."

"They're in your pocket," Jed told him bitterly. "You could begin printing more counterfeit
bills with them as soon as you got out of Boston. You
could begin printing them tonight if you wanted.
What good are fifty thousand pounds of bills to the
Major if you still have the plates?"

"Now Jed . . ."

"You planned it this way from the start," Jed
cried. "You've never intended turning honest. It's the
only way you could think of to get your printing
press through the American lines. That's all that
matters to you—getting your press out of Boston so
you can go right on printing counterfeit rebel money
for the British. Well, I can't stop you from going but
I won't let you take those printing plates you've got.
Give them to me, sir."

Mr. Box sadly shook his head. "Hovey always
said you were too honest for us. With your brains it
seems a fearful waste!" He drew a pistol from his
pocket. "But waste or not, don't try to stop me,
m'boy, for as you can see, I'm armed."

"I don't care," Jed told him, and began walking
toward him across the snow. "Go ahead and shoot
me. It will bring Major Duncan running, and he'll
put you in jail, which is more than I can bring myself to do."

"Ah, Jed, m'boy," said Mr. Box sadly, "I can't
shoot you, noise or no noise—I'd as soon shoot myself. Take the stupid plates." He threw them across
the snow. "You're a fool for believing these ragged
rebels of yours can win—yes, and I'm a bigger fool

for growing fond of you." He tucked the pistol into his belt and gave Jed a rueful smile. "You would have made a wonderful counterfeiter, m'boy, if only you didn't have that rotten streak of honesty in you." He sighed. "I fear you'll never get ahead in this world —it's a pity."

"I'll miss you, Mr. Box," Jed told him soberly.

"Thank you, m'boy. I'll be going now, and I don't mind saying I'll miss you, too. If ever you see a sign saying 'Titherming Box, Printer and Engraver' —why, stop in for a cup of tea and a warm welcome, m'boy." With these words he pulled himself over the wall and vanished among the trees.

Jed stood staring after him for a long time. When Major Duncan found him there were tears on his cheeks.

"Where have you been?" asked the major quietly. "We looked all over the house for you. The plates!" he gasped, seeing them scattered across the snow. "He had the engraving plates, too?"

"Aye," said Jed sadly. "He had them all the time and never intended giving them to you! He never intended to become an honest man, either. All he wanted was the pass to get him and his printing press through the lines."

"Jacoby—Morse!" shouted the major. "See if you can find the man!"

Jed turned to him with a sob. "Oh, Major, it's my fault he's gone, but I couldn't betray him. He was kind to me—the first person who was kind to me. I made him give up the plates, but I couldn't stop his going. And now he'll make new plates and print more counterfeit money, I know he will—and it'll be my doing, because I let him go."

The major put his arm across Jed's shoulder. "Nay, lad, you can't say what he'll do. Perhaps from knowing you, Jed, he'll bend a little with a new wind and become a better man. Well, Jacoby?" he asked, glancing up at his corporal.

"Not a sign of him, Major Duncan. Morse has gone to the town gates to see if he can catch him there."

The major nodded. "I doubt that we'll see him again, but thanks to Jed we have the plates. In the meantime—" He looked down at Jed with a wry smile. "In the meantime, lad, the Widow Muffet has a chicken roasting over the fire for us."

"Yes, sir," said Jed, still dazed.

"Come along, now. You and I have a long war ahead of us to win. There's work to be done."

"Yes, sir," said Jed, and blew his nose. He glanced once more at the wall over which Mr. Box had disappeared. He guessed that Mr. Box had gotten away safely. He guessed that Mr. Box would *always* get away safely. He was, after all, a man who believed first in landing on his feet.

With a nod Jed turned to the major. "I'm with you, sir," he said, and gratefully fell into step beside him.

End

DOROTHY GILMAN BUTTERS

Mrs. Butters was born in New Brunswick, New Jersey, and has been interested in writing since the tender age of twelve when she produced a monthly magazine (circulation thirteen copies; price five cents). Her only serious digression was in the field of art where her work at the Pennsylvania Academy of Fine Arts was rewarded by a Cresson Scholarship. The author, her educator husband and two sons live near Lake Hiawatha, New Jersey.

TITLE II